The Vatican Games

Alejandra Guibert

Clink Street

London | New York

Published by Clink Street Publishing 2019

Copyright © 2019

First edition.

paperback ISBN: 978-1-913136-30-7
ebook ISBN: 978-1-913136-31-4

The *new* World gives the sensation of Light, of life, of all-pervading consciousness, of joy... But to *a mind which is not prepared* the same world will give a sensation of infinite darkness and terror.

P.D. Ouspensky

PART I

The sky was in mourning, covered by a blanket of black smoke rising from the millions of corpses. They were too many to bury. Satellite photos showed only a few scattered green or white areas standing out like oases. The incineration of the bodies imposed a universal state of mourning which nobody would ever forget or openly mention again.

Multinationals would at last be able to focus fully on business, they would have free rein to do and undo as they pleased in their new kingdom. Hunger had been eradicated. Not by the philanthropic efforts of the few humanitarians still harbouring a vision for the future of humanity, nor through the generosity of the wealthy. Hunger had been eliminated once and for all. With the death of nearly five billion people.

The stars were rising above the horizon at the moment of her birth. The cosmos surrounded her in silent protection, unbeknown to her. All the planets were present, aligned like a fan, spread out before her eyes, which she half opened in curiosity. Her position, date and time of birth in relation to the cosmos were unique. Coincidence or not, they matched a physical anomaly which put her life in danger from her very first breath.

There she was, at the centre, without having wished it. She had been born.

The doctor visited her mother in the ward where she was recovering. It was not a routine visit. He had received detailed reports of the past few days. He had seen her clinical records and had been called in to give his expert opinion. Straight away he identified the condition. He explained it to her in simple terms.

'A gap between the left and right hemispheres is normal in any new-born baby. In her case it is larger than usual.'

Encephalitis due to hydrocephaly, water on the brain. It was the first time he had ignored the ethics he always followed with his patients. Honesty above all. What good could come of telling this hopeful young girl the truth when she had barely emerged from hell. The neurologist knew her daughter would not survive but kept it to himself. He advised her to protect the baby's head as best she could.

The first thing Alina did was register the birth. With her brand new name Vera spent days under observation until she was discharged a week later. It was only a matter of time. They could do nothing further for her and they could not keep her there. The Neurological Hospital was a hive of activity. Time became crucial with each passing hour. Vera had ceased to be a priority. Alina did not hold this against them; on the contrary, she was grateful, though to everyone there, this might have seemed bizarre. Once she had left, Alina felt free from the pressing sense of danger. She remembered the nurse's words:

'Lots of things are happening. You're better off not knowing. You must rest and look after your baby.'

The instructions were clear.

She started to knit a perfect circle, which she measured meticulously every three or four rows. In the meantime, as a precaution she folded a handkerchief in four and tied it with a ribbon to Vera's head. Vera undid it in no time, lifting her arm to get rid of the bothersome ribbon. Each time Alina checked on her daughter she would find Vera chewing at the handkerchief by her side with her tender head now bare. Unprotected. She seemed to smile when she managed to get rid of the handkerchief. Her playful challenge did not distract Alina from her task. Eventually she lifted up the knitted cotton skullcap, smooth and perfect; convinced that it would protect her baby girl.

'Look. Don't you like it? Don't take it off, sweetheart.'

She sewed on the ribbon, which Vera strummed like guitar strings and admired the result as though she were an expert in Renaissance headware. This time it took her a little over an hour to remove the handmade helmet tied to her ears.

'It wasn't my idea. The doctor told me to do it. Why won't you leave it alone?' Alina asked her.

Alina watched her intently. Although she tried to understand what was bothering her daughter, what she wanted most was to persuade the child with her eyes of the danger Vera appeared not to notice. It was practically impossible for her to contemplate that Vera might not understand her words. The way Vera looked at her said the opposite. Or was she the one who could not comprehend what her baby was trying to tell her?

She paced up and down in front of the window, anxiously covering Vera's head with only her hand for protection over the soft skin. She crossed back and forth from one wall to the other cradling Vera, murmuring anxious maternal nothings. She thought aloud of a way to protect the door, which remained open as if there were some plan that continually put her daughter in danger. Alina whispered questions to her as though Vera could provide the answer. 'Why don't you want it? Does it bother you? Is it too tight? Look how soft it is. Vera, tell me. What else can I do? Tell me, sweetheart.'

The window of her room was the only respite for Alina, a few minutes' truce to distract her from the pressure she would be under once again. The danger which, try as she might, she could not push away. When the intensity of her thoughts exhausted her, having no clear purpose but more as a spontaneous reaction for self-preservation, Alina would stop at the window to distance herself from her thoughts. For hours she would repeat the same cycle. The longer she spent trying to find a solution, the longer her time at the window. These were precious minutes where life outside was so unreal that it became spellbinding. Vera also appreciated a break from her mother's repetitive mumblings, from her overwhelming concern and her toing and froing like a caged beast. Vera would wave her arms in delight at the visits to the window. The neighbour's little boy kept throwing his white rubber ball up in the air into a spin. It popped in and out of view as if the boy were on a mission to entertain the baby girl or her mother. Each throw brought forth a squeal of pleasure from Vera. It not only drew a fresh smile on Alina's face, it also pulled her out from under her cloud of apprehension. Mother and daughter followed the ball's hypnotic rise and fall for a long while, until it fell to the ground with a thud, shaking Alina out of her stupor. Perhaps Vera might have the answer for her after all. It was what she had unintentionally wished for. When she opened the window wide the boy had already disappeared inside the building.

With the precise shape of her baby's head in mind, Alina slipped downstairs with renewed determination. When the neighbour opened the door she found Alina there, emotionless like a Madonna. The child clinging to his mother's skirt eyed the visitor with distrust. Alina asked to see the ball and he hugged it with the same love with which she would cradle Vera in her arms. On taking it into her open hand Alina knew. The boy turned towards his mother in confusion, sensing the worst. The conspiratorial look of both mothers and their nodding heads were unequivocal. Although the neighbour tried to explain to him in the best way she could, the boy refused to give up his ball, let alone allow it to be cut in two. He somehow managed to transform his compulsion to burst into tears into a stern composure. The three looked at each other for a few seconds, floundering in a silence which offered no escape. Having no desire to intervene, Vera merely observed the cobwebs that held together the dilapidated walls of the corridor. The meeting in the doorway had reached an impasse. The silent seconds stretched almost into minutes, until Vera suddenly invaded the adults' quiet with a squeal of pleasure as though she were seeing the ball in the air. A timely intervention that inspired in Alina a promising idea, which not only would it preserve the integrity of a little boy and his ball, but would endow it with new meaning. The boy looked again at his mother, who opened her eyes wide to give him the assurance he was hoping for. His eyes had a new fire in them, which she had never seen before. The promise of a new ball of his choosing sent a sudden tingle through his body. It was a feeling repeated shortly after, when Alina presented him with the money served on the remaining half of the ball like a platter. In no time at all, the boy had become an accomplice. It was his half ball on top of Vera's head. A ribbon through two strategically perforated holes at each end tied it down at ear level. A life-saving skull-cap which Vera would no longer be able to pull off.

On their return visit to the hospital a few weeks later, the nurse accompanied them to Neurology. Her footsteps echoed against the walls as she entered the room carrying

Vera like the announcement of a portent to the waiting neurologist and surrounding people. Once more she was the centre of attention. Alina removed the helmet she had made with the rubber ball, a dear belonging of the little boy, now uplifted with pride.

'I'm taking Vera to hospital today. She'll be wearing your ball,' she had said to the boy as if she were taking her to a party wearing a new dress.

'Can I come too?'

'No. I'll tell you all about it later.'

The neurologist looked solemn as he invited the two doctors by his side to attest to the miracle of Vera's open crown. Alina's proximity forced the experts to mumble unintelligibly. She turned from one to the other trying to understand the seriousness of what they were saying. Time and again Alina offered them the rubber cap, fearing for her daughter's bare head suspended between their fine fingers. Once Vera was back in the neurologist's arms, he nodded to her mother, who approached, relieved, and put the solid protector back on. It was Vera who once again intervened, this time with a string of gurgles to ease the situation, her apologetic mother giggling her approval. The neurologist passed her from one hand to the other to examine her reflexes. He pulled her little legs, which were receptive to each flexion or extension. Vera responded to the cold thumb on her spine and to the taps of a hammer larger than her diminutive hands on her tiny red knees. The doctors and students in the room were stunned as they saw for themselves just how healthy the baby girl was. Not only was it a miracle that Vera was alive, but also that she remained unaffected by the fluid invading her cranial interstices. It did not seem to alter in the least her reflexes or state of alertness. On the contrary, Vera was enjoying all the fuss at the hands of the three doctors as they passed her between them like modelling clay.

Before the year was up, Vera's miracle had begun to fade away. When one night she began to pat herself on the rubber shell, Alina knew it was time to take it off. With one hand at either side steadying her head she noted that the valley which had kept both hemispheres apart had completely closed over, sealing the danger. She had succeeded in her task, now she could rest. The half ball, which had survived unscathed, could also rest from Vera's scratching among the other pieces on Alina's altar: the vase, the candle, the picture of Saint Genevieve, and the Polaroid photo of Alina, taken by the flour mill's foreman in the wheat field days before the birth.

When Alina left hospital a week after giving birth, she felt as though years rather than days had gone by since the flour mill and life on the farm. Recent events had unfolded at the speed of dreams or nightmares. The reality of the previous few years had dragged on for her at a leaden pace, which made the present all the more inconceivable. The life she had been so looking forward to was taking on a new shape. She had wanted with all her might to bring up her daughter away from the farm. She had not imagined that the world would suffer a catastrophic transformation so that that which was inexplicable and yet marvellous ended up replacing the adversity of her past. Vera had been born through danger. She had already overcome the most traumatic day in the history of humanity. She was to grow up in ignorance of the miracle of her survival. Vera and her inestimable core: barely covered by a veil of flesh, permeable to the wisdom of the cosmos. She had overcome death before she was born. When her mother began her contractions, the cataclysm which was to take place minutes before Vera was born had just been unleashed.

The monoplane had flown over the reconnaissance area for the second time. The truck which was to have picked up the field workers had never reached its destination. Alina's shouting was inaudible from the aircraft flying above, counting the dead. From the sky the pilot struggled to count the stiff bodies strewn over the wheat extending to either side of the flour mill.

With her handkerchief over her mouth Alina ran despite her advanced state of pregnancy. She ran towards the truck in the distance, fleeing from the bodies scattered in her way like crumbs left by characters from a children's story. Her eyes opened wide in agony, she tried not to look around her. Her legs, weighed down by her condition, responded to the adrenaline and her determination to give birth. Her right hand was opened out like a wing lovingly supporting the new life she had harboured for almost nine months. Her movements were awkward. The ground seemed to resist the primal urgency which warned her of danger. She felt the occasional whipping of the ears of wheat on the hand with which she protected her face every time she raised her head so as not to lose sight of the distant truck, which gradually became larger, distracting her from the array of sacrificial bodies. A few metres more and they would be safe. Each step essential. She waved her arm like a flag among the wheat, fearing that the driver would not wait for her; now he should be able to see her from the truck, even if he could not hear her. She approached the truck in the middle of the dirt road, which cut through the high wheat fields. In the deathly silence her smile became a scream reaching the baby in her warm maternal sack. The amniotic fluid froze as did the blood in her body, which had until now been a welcoming place. She leant against the static truck to calm the irregular pulse which began throbbing in her temples. Through the window, two lifeless bodies remained seated before the windscreen as though admiring a golden landscape.

Alina went into labour, just like an animal she pushed without pause. The passing hours brought no respite in her efforts nor did they show her an easier path. She had seen the animals on the farm give birth. It seemed so natural. She became accustomed to the cycle of pushing and pain. Each attempt seemed to open her up a few millimetres more. She bent forwards to find that what seemed like a tear barely revealed a few centimetres of skin which was not her own. On touching the soft fuzz which announced the baby's arrival she could not tell whether it was joy or fear that brought tears to her eyes.

Everything appeared to come to a halt until her baby slipped over the sacks on which she sat every day with her workmates on their way to work in the fields. At last mother and daughter rested, snuggling together against all discomfort. With her baby in her arms she watched the pale moon already visible in the last light of the evening; the full moon, which would soon swathe the newborn Vera protectively in blue, was about to rise.

It was the black smoke behind the truck that alerted the aeroplane on its second reconnaissance flight. Alina woke up on the wooden floor. She was sore all over. Nothing could compare to the burning feeling inside and out; so it had not been a dream. It felt damp between her legs. She reached down, ran her hand through the birth secretions and wiped it on the wooden floor. In the very place where she believed she had dreamt she had given birth, she awoke to the certainty of the baby by her side. She also awoke to the events which had made Vera's arrival so fraught in the same natural way in which she had given birth. Those events were demanding her full attention.

Tying the corners of a sack to the truck, she shaded Vera from the sun which was beginning to burn. She managed to unhook the spare wheel, roll it behind the truck and set it alight a few metres away in the middle of the road. The aeroplane approached as the smoke started billowing like a flock of black birds. If she could distinguish human figures inside the aeroplane, then they could surely see her standing with her arms in the air next to the burning wheel. Exhausted but happy, Alina hurried to her baby to tell her they would soon be rescued. She lay down next to the child, listening out for the sound of the engine. She tried not to succumb to the sleepiness induced by sheer relief at their imminent rescue. To combat her drowsiness she climbed down from the truck every so often to look through the cab window at the dashboard clock, enough to restart the cycle of anxiety which she thought was over. Shaded from the sun by the improvised canopy, for Alina the long hours of waiting became as drawn out as her thirst. The fear which came over her in waves was superseded by long intervals of lethargy. But, her mind totally blank, she could still be dazzled by each and every inch of Vera's tiny body and immersing herself in its contemplation pulled her out of her uneasiness.

Even if in Alina's mind nothing could justify the silence, the inaction, the abandonment, the aeroplane's orders had been clear. They were to report accurately on the situation. They were not there to save lives.

Her water bottle was empty. It had been a relief that Vera had begun to feed almost immediately, but now the sense of calm was fading away with each visit she made to the cab window. With her face pressed against the glass Alina now peered eagerly into the cab, looking for something to drink. It was littered with soft drink cans, all empty and flattened like paper in the men's fists as though in defiance before rigor mortis set in. Cans which had arrived in the local town of Abriola, well-timed to coincide with the heat wave. The driver and his assistant had drained them one after another courtesy of the sponsor of the local festival. Everyone had something, except Alina, whose early nausea had made sure she abstained from sweet drinks since the onset of her pregnancy. Now she was driven by the memory of the fizzing sound as the cans were opened and the image of the liquid she had refused pouring down people's throats. The GMO company from Missouri had generously left dozens of boxes of soft drinks for distribution among the villagers. They had organised a festival to celebrate the first harvest of GM wheat, from the first crop to which the flour company had agreed. The work was temporary but well paid and they had taken her on in spite of her pregnancy. Alina had shown them her toughened hands. The foreman knew her and had known her father. He knew she was a strong worker in spite of her young age. Above all he wanted to help her. It was obvious that things had changed on the farm since her father's death. The family no longer attended Abriola's festivities. The pregnancy had also been a surprise and rumours had begun to circulate. When he saw her in the queue of job applicants the foreman knew right away he would let her have the job. He did not care what people would say. As long as the pregnancy did not interfere with her work, everything would be fine. Alina would go into the wheat fields with another sixteen labourers before harvest time to supervise and tend to the genetically modified wheat ears.

By the afternoon Alina had managed to forget about the inert bodies in the cab. She climbed down to pick some ears of wheat. She chewed the almost ripe grains while she covered Vera with the lower part of her skirt which she had torn off with her teeth. In the same way she had cut the umbilical cord which joined her to her baby, whom she now gave to the world. As if knowing already of Vera's extreme vulnerability, Alina covered her head with her handkerchief. She waited a second night for the rescuers while the full moon, now shining brightly high up in the sky, nourished Vera's calm sleep. Holding her daughter in her arms Alina pulled the empty sacks over the two of them, yearning for another dawn.

The following morning Vera was in the same position in

her arms. Still clinging to her breast, suckling from time to time, letting go only to sleep. There they were, the truck, the dead, the burnt tyre no longer smoking. Nobody had come to rescue them. Nobody would come. Alina ate a few more wheat grains, while she looked Vera over and twisted her skirt into a point to remove the occasional remains of dried blood from the folds of the baby's skin. Having eaten Alina regained the confidence she had lost. Now she was certain that if she waited for help they would die. First her, probably, and then her baby once her breast had dried up completely. She herself would have to save them both. How? was the question in her mind. She could not even drive a car, let alone a truck. She first made sure Vera had a good feed and left her asleep in the shade of the canopy. She tore off the sleeve of her T-shirt, tied it at the nape of her neck like a surgical mask and jumped down from the truck. In one swift movement Alina opened the cab door, apologising as she did so. Without looking at him she tugged at the shirt of the driver, who fell stiffly onto the dry ground. She struggled into his seat and stared ahead, trying not to look at the co-driver. The smell was only just bearable. She hardly breathed, not because of the stench coming from the body beside her – she was used to strong smells on her mother's farm – but because of the stillness which had built up overnight in the cab; an inertia which she could not define but could only be overcome with the composure of that protective instinct which now drove her to act. She looked around the dashboard and, though not understanding much, she did recognise the pedals and the gear lever. But she had no idea in what order to use them.

'It'll be all right... it'll be all right', she told herself when she shut her eyes and turned the key which responded instantly. It was the familiar, encouraging sound of the running engine. Alina could almost feel her father's presence with clear images of him at the wheel. She tried to evoke the movements, the sequence of steps. She knew that in order to move the gear lever she had to depress one of the pedals. It had been many years since her father had allowed her to change gears in the pickup when the family went out for a drive on Sundays. Even if she had looked to see which pedal he used, she would not be able to remember now. She would have to try them one at a time. The right-hand pedal increased the engine noise but the truck remained stationary. The middle pedal did not allow any movement of the gear lever at all. To move the lever she clearly had to step on the pedal on the left. The anticipation of driving her baby to safety herself thrilled her. She took a deep breath, depressed the clutch pedal and went into first gear. Alina was about to step on the accelerator, half-closing her eyes, when she released the clutch. The liberating sound of the engine became hostile. The whole truck shook before falling into its previous silence broken only by Vera's inconsolable crying. She had no idea why it had not worked. The body next to her was now pressing against her shoulder and all her earlier courage drained away. Then with a huge jump Alina launched herself from the cab onto the dusty ground, hard enough to make her ankle twist with the fall. Frustrated by her efforts and troubled by her daughter's cry, Alina wept for the first time. She could not think for thirst and pain. Cradling Vera in her arms, the precious fluid of her tears fell onto her baby's tiny hands as she stroked them between her fingers. In an effort to console both herself and her baby she rocked back and forth. She let Vera suckle barely the last drops of life she could offer her, feeling the warm, humid mouth on her breast as she sealed her own dry lips. If only she had something to drink. If she could drink… Against all odds it struck her that the only hope might be among the corpses she had left behind so she retraced her steps. A rubbish bag hanging from a post near an entrance to the wheat field swayed slightly. At the end of the day's work the labourers disposed of their empty cans or other litter in it before leaving the field. They had not finished work that day. The cans must be with their owners, fallen like them onto the dry ground. If any liquid was left in the cans next to the bodies it would have dried up from the heat. Absurd as it seemed, each prone body encouraged the hope that she might find something to drink. She was glad she barely knew those pale faces with their gaping mouths against the ground.

Despite her eighteen years, Alina rarely visited Abriola. She had seldom left her mother's farm and only then in the company of her mother and her new husband – the man who had replaced her father overnight. Although years had gone by since her father's death, she would always see him as the new husband who forbade everything and demanded it all. Each year the young girl witnessed the unmentionable, her eyes incredulous. That man would never be her father. Her unexpected pregnancy had deepened her need to seek other possibilities. It had not been easy for her to convince him to let her apply for the job at the flour mill. Alina was aware that they needed the extra income. No words were necessary. She knew all too well what life would be like for her child on the farm. The new husband controlled the money they spent, the work they did, the time to rest, the time to go out, their joys and sorrows – the latter always plentiful. He also controlled the frequency of the beatings to which he had been subjecting the two women for the past seven years. Alina did not want Vera to be born there. She would take her last few weeks' pay and leave for the city. She had saved what little money the man would give her out of her salary, 'For the baby boy,' he had said to her, 'it's going to be a boy.' 'Once I've left the mill' was all Alina could think of. The foreman at the flour mill had found her a job, working for a recently widowed old lady. The pay was not much but the main thing was to get away from the farm. The foreman asked no questions and would give no answers. The simplicity of their tacit understanding was an unexpected blessing compared to the risk inherent in her intentions. A risk which became almost negligible when viewed from the wheat field. Now her plans seemed so distant, belonging to another reality on which she must not dwell if she hoped to save her child.

Under the weighty body only the strap of the cloth bag was visible to the side. Alina put down her walking stick and tugged at the canvas until she saw the bulky bag. A further hefty pull shook the stiff corpse. Again she apologised as she crossed herself. The can in the bag was unopened. The lifeless body had sheltered it from the intense heat. The sugar in the fizzy drink would give her the necessary energy to face the twelve-mile walk back to the mill. As Alina opened the can and put it to her lips, the sound of engines in the distance made her look up. The blue sky was cloudless and empty, but in the distance a familiar cloud of dust was travelling towards the truck. The noise was not of an aeroplane but of a vehicle approaching by land. Providentially she dropped the can onto the ground, the foamy brown liquid running into the wheat, just like her. Without her walking stick, clutching her tender and painful loins, Alina strode back as best she could to reach Vera, whom she had left sleeping under the canopy on the truck.

Dressed in white from head to toe, the men arrived in several vehicles to remove the bodies. The extraordinary events took on a new dimension for Alina, when she saw the men wearing transparent bell-like covers over their heads. Avoiding any physical contact they took her away in a sealed van. She was instructed to lie on a stretcher. When they tried to take Vera away she would not let them in spite of having little strength left to object to anything. After giving her a few sips of water, a male nurse explained that she would not yet be able to eat anything. They needed to carry out several blood tests to confirm that she was not in danger. Another nurse informed her they would give her oxygen in order to take blood. They were not only exceedingly careful but they were also very kind. For a moment she felt like the most important person in the world. She did not expect them to be taking blood every fifteen minutes in tiny tubes on which they marked the exact time. Nor could she imagine at any point that she would be taken by plane to the Bioterrorism Research Centre. She simply did not even know where she was or why.

On the plane she was isolated in a special cabin. Here two nurses would measure her vital signs each time they took blood to monitor her state. They would record the results, later sealing them in a plastic envelope together with the samples. They only took blood from Vera twice since Alina objected when she started crying forcefully the second time.

Several doctors were awaiting them at the Centre. Some spoke in a strange language and only addressed Alina to give her instructions or tell her briefly what they were going to do. The assistants went back and forth with the plastic envelopes containing the blood samples of mother and daughter. When someone else tried again to take away the baby girl, Alina would not allow them to. It was only then that they sutured the umbilical cord, bathed her, measured and weighed her in the lab. She set as a condition for their attending to her that Vera was to have someone beside her to look after her at all times. To Alina, who had always had conditions imposed on her, it felt strange to have her demands accepted without question. They were eventually moved to a private room where Alina was able to shower. From the shower she could see Vera asleep in her cot. In barely forty-eight hours her life had changed from a daily nightmare to another, far more extreme and unreal. Now from the safety of her bed Alina took pleasure in looking back on it like a film. It was a luxury to be able to smile at her daughter for the first time since she had been born.

She was unaware that many had died in Abriola. A nurse in a standard uniform gave her a white night-dress and brought her some chicken soup. She could also speak good Italian. These were the first clear signs of safety and Alina was at last able to sleep without interruption. Her deep sleep prevented her dreams from surfacing and being remembered. In an instinctive effort to avoid any further turmoil, she had preferred not to know. But when she woke up the nurse's expression made her feel the need to ask:

'Do you know what happened to those people in the wheat fields?'

'Don't worry about that. You must rest.'

'You don't want to tell me, or did they tell you not to say anything?'

'You lost a lot of blood during the birth.'

'I feel all right. Where are we?'

'Saint Louis, Missouri.' By Alina's blank expression, the nurse realised these names didn't mean anything to her. 'America. Nobody knows why, but people are dying. That's what they say on the news. They brought in all those who'd been with you in the field to find out what happened. You two are OK. All the tests were negative.'

This information was enough for her to ask when she could leave, prompting a neurologist to appear, dressed in everyday clothes, to examine Vera's skull. Through the nurse he asked her where she lived and explained she would be transferred to a specialist hospital back home in Italy. Alina just showed him the piece of paper with the old lady´s address in the city of Bari written on it. He gave her some money she did not expect. With it she set out on a new journey to leave memories behind.

Scientists continued to analyse the dozens of blood samples from Alina, seeking some exceptional antibody able to resist what had annihilated everyone else. They had found in the blood of the dead traces of atropine, an anticholinergic agent which had blocked their central and peripheral nervous systems. Its action was like closing a heavy hatch and locking it by turning the wheel with the combination lock. Whoever had extracted the atropine from belladonna, the most toxic plant in the western hemisphere, knew that a single leaf of the plant is fatal. For the compound they had obviously used the much more toxic root. The experts knew it had to be a compound. The report from the US stated that it was cattle and horses that had died initially. Scientists were perplexed, knowing that cattle were immune to belladonna. They needed to find an isolated sample of the compound that could be hiding its other components in blood. But nothing was hidden in either Vera or her mother's blood. They were the only ones in the wheat fields who had escaped being infected. If only they had asked Alina, she could have told them that the people in Abriola had been suffering under the terrible heat. That for days the villagers had done nothing but guzzle soft drinks which arrived with the sponsorship. If they had only asked her she could have told them that she had drunk nothing but water. They would not find anything in her blood samples. The only answer was in the blood of the dead.

The flight back seemed too long now that she knew she was going home. It was her first time in a city. There was an ambulance waiting for them at Bari airport. The neurologist at the University Neurological Hospital also predicted that Vera would not survive the night. After five nights a nurse told her they had to free up the hospital bed.

With the money they had given her at the Centre Alina rented a room in a hostel near the old lady's house to start her new life. If everything went to plan the old lady would return in a few weeks from her brother's house where her husband's funeral had been held. The only thing she could do was wait. Everything would be different there. She would be free of the ordeal of the farm. Vera was her only chance of freedom.

In the press the news came out before any real knowledge of the compound was available or the experts had precise scientific facts to report. Tabloids all over the world speculated as usual. They first broke the shock news, revelling in the sordid details. In other sections of the media, parallels to Greek mythology readily inspired the intellectuals as soon as one of the toxic elements was found, 'atropine'. One article read: 'Ironically, its name comes from the Greek "Atropos", the eldest of the three goddesses of destiny, known for being inflexible and inevitable. According to Greek mythology the fate of human beings was in the hands of the three sisters. Clotho spun the thread of life, Lachesis measured it and Atropos chose the time and manner to cut the thread. The distributors of destiny were the managers of the thread of life. Are we dealing with the manifestation of a Machiavellian intrigue planned with expert sadism? Or is it simply a monstrous coincidence?'

After a few days the articles gave way to lists of people and places and to reports on where to go to incinerate the bodies of relatives or neighbours. There were no more plays on words. Reality had gone beyond fantasy. Telephone lines became overloaded hampering order and facilitating chaos. People were asked to remain in their homes during the night and to go to work during the day. Carry on as usual, implored the authorities. Messages on the national networks announced, reminded, urged people to carry on with life in the midst of death.

Many in Abriola had died but the contamination there had not spread. Now the world knew why. The cans of soft drink that killed the people in the field it emerged had come directly from the United States, where deaths were numbering almost 150,000 in just a few days. Alina had not been told any of this. Nobody knew that many more deaths were on the horizon. Unthinkable figures.

Terrorists were believed to have contaminated a soft

drinks plant in Atlanta. In New York three billion gallons of drinking water a day were distributed to the households of over twenty million inhabitants through a network of twenty-two reservoirs and five controlled lakes. In the Newtown Creek plant in Brooklyn, processing 500 million gallons of water a day, the most horrific plague also broke out. New York was a mere example of what was to come in the whole of the American territory and beyond.

Through drinking water systems from surface water streams, rainwater distribution systems, rivers, lakes, the sewerage system, septic fields, waste water ducts, storm drains, reservoirs. Through water treatment plants, with capacity of twenty million gallons a day. By way of biosolids or sediment made into fertilizer. For their use in sown fields which had also received water from irrigated fields. In each and every one of these the poison lay in wait. Contaminated water emerged from the sewers straight into the rivers and streams. The cycle was infinitely renewed. Although water was being analysed, it was months before it was possible to correctly identify the agent that was poisoning the population. Meanwhile, nobody knew what to do with the contaminated waters that flowed murky or crystalline with the new poison in other outlets, other drains, other fountains in major cities of the USA.

The police, the emergency coordinators for each State, finally issued a red alert by radio and TV. The terrorist alert was severe, although apart from being bacteriological, it was not clear what the threat was. There were no areas to be evacuated because it seemed to affect them all. As a preventive measure some schools were turned into shelters, simply to accommodate children whose parents did not come home or did so to die. In the shelters there were provisions, nurses, police. Nobody could guarantee protection.

The undoable had been done in the simplest way. In only eight American cities, little bags had been thrown carelessly into rivers, sewers, reservoirs and dissolved in a matter of minutes on contact with water. They were filled with poison designed with DNA synthesis technology. Science had gone beyond itself. Years of research, millions invested in progress, the brilliant minds of the experts, and the hunger for scientific advancement had resulted in the efficient synthesis of pathogenic genomes. This great discovery had given free rein to a new pocket Frankenstein.

The basis of the murderous compound was botulinum. The toxin used in the infamous Botox, advertised and adored by celebrities fearful of the sagging of unsupported flesh, killed millions at a stroke. In small doses it had become the most famous invention for cosmetic treatment, smoothing out wrinkles in a few hours by preventing muscular contraction. But for the purpose of terrorism in a matter of hours it induced respiratory failure, paralysis of the body and death. Rather more than a facial injection. Victims' faces, frozen in a contorted expression could no longer be compared to the smiles of the fans of Botox. This world Botox party had been organised by young terrorists not the least interested in the world of fashion. The bacteria in the compound would continue to grow and develop, preventing its destruction or elimination for decades.

In Bari, the community of Poor Clares was so shaken by the alarming news that they did not even dare to drink the water from their own well. The Mother Superior decided to call Father Zillo. He was not only their mentor, but the founder of the new community. Ten years earlier he had saved the Santa Chiara convent from closure, following an infamous brawl between the Mother Superior and three resident nuns. The violent nuns were transferred putting an end to the disputes, leaving the Archbishop with little choice but to close the convent building.

'All convents are necessary,' Father Zillo had insisted to

the Archbishop. 'A closed convent is a historical monument, an open one is a home for worship and the opportunity for new callings.'

The Archbishop agreed with the priest's logic, although he still thought his solution to the problem was a little peculiar.

'Archbishop, the Convent of San Leonardo de Montefalco is overpopulated. If I may, I intend to nominate a Mother Superior from there who will choose the nuns who wish to go with her.'

Father Zillo soon found new residents for Santa Chiara at Bari. Mother Teresa, chosen as the new Mother Superior, arrived along with twelve sisters. Sister Benedita was the last to be chosen. Sister Leopoldina had nominated her, although sister Eulalia and other nuns who had already been accepted by Mother Teresa had their doubts, due to Benedita's young age and impulsive personality. But they all trusted Mother Teresa and were grateful for having the chance to start together their own community in a historic convent building like Santa Chiara. Their enthusiasm was too holy to reject a keen applicant like Benedita, and Mother Teresa reminded them to be united in their task of sanctifying through their behavior a place that had been disrespected by its previous occupants.

As financial investor for the Vatican, father Zillo even volunteered to take care of the "nitty-gritty" of the formalities, as he had put it to the Archbishop. Being from Bari himself, father Zillo had a special attachment to the monasteries and churches he had been brought up to admire, and was determined to help the Poor Clares settle down in their new monastic life. He had developed a weakness for the newly formed community. When Mother Teresa called him that morning, he had already advised them to stay in the convent until which time he could return from Rome to join them.

'I've asked Sister Benedita not to go out, but she doesn't

listen. It's now the second time she's sneaked out to help at the health centre.'

'Reverend Mother, we're witnessing the unwitnessable.'

The detailed information Zillo was receiving from the Vatican showed it was mainly in the US where bodies were piling up like carcasses.

'We know the scope of contamination is immeasurable. We live a life of retreat, Father, and I cannot allow Sister Benedita to be exposed to risk.'

'Above all, we must remain calm, Reverend Mother. I'm on my way.'

Father Zillo reached Bari to find that Benedita had left the convent early.

'Sisters, I have specific news. Contagion between humans is not possible.'

'It's the water, Father. Everything is contaminated… everything depends on water. The poison can reach any of us,' Sister Eulalia rubbed her reddened hands.

'I know. They're investigating the sources. We must all remain calm.'

'People are dropping like flies. The roads are blocked by cars with drivers dead at the wheel! Airplanes full of passengers have dropped out of the skies!' Despite her best efforts, Sister Eulalia could not control herself. Sister Leopoldina's embrace helped her contain the shaking which had taken over her body, while she struggled to suppress the fright which came out of her in short whimpers.

'Those reports come from abroad, Sister. The situation here is less serious.'

The sisters spent Christmas in prayer, living on minimal rations sourced from the vegetable garden. They could not be sure, but the water from the well was their best chance of avoiding contamination. There was no reason why it should contain the poison, Father Zillo had concluded. Sister Benedita continued to help out at the health centres, with the blessing of the Mother Superior. As long as she took a lunch box and bottle of well-water.

On American territory death was striking in quick, merciless succession. With the threat of cholera looming, ovens were quickly installed for instant incineration. Bodies with wallets in their pockets, with photos of their loved ones, with credit cards and driving licences, club and store cards. So much burning plastic relieving the sinister smell of burnt flesh. Some had barely learnt to recognise the signs in others before symptoms began to appear in their own body: lack of coordination, increased body temperature, photophobia, blurred vision, palpitations, confusion, sometimes vomiting and then the final collapse. Death on every corner. As if a ghostly exterminator invisibly brushed past its victims. The uncertainty while waiting for a relative. The certainty of hours without any news. Confirmation at the end of the day. Fear of falling victim oneself at any moment. Those who were helping to pile up corpses, to transport or incinerate them; those who had miraculously survived the cataclysm could not escape the bitter punishment of remembering the dead, the dying, bodies strewn all over the place. There would be no need of monuments for their collective memory to share the horror that lived on privately in the minds of the survivors.

After a few weeks, searching for the terrorists became as pointless as it was absurd. They could easily be among the dead – among the hundreds of thousands impossible to identify for lack of time. It was a *déjà vu* of 11th September – when, despite the most basic security measures, the towers collapsed before the world's eyes like crumbling sandcastles. Everybody wondered where were the operating systems, the preventive measures, the planning, the hundreds of employees and strategists, the scientists, the millions of dollars invested in defence programmes. This time, when the alarms sounded, everyone started running around in their offices like headless chickens while the millions of unemployed or the destitute in the south fell like black flies, their open mouths hitting the dust roads where long-promised asphalt had never materialised. The failings of organisational bureaucracy were there for all to see. Mobile supply points and emergency shelters were of no use. People were still dying in the shelters. Police and fire-fighting departments were hard pushed to coordinate their efforts to keep public order and provide a minimum level of assistance. All shelters were eventually closed down and individuals were left to their own devices.

On the other side of the Atlantic, Alina spent her days in the rented room, getting to know her daughter and learning how to look after her. Vera's fragility made her mother apprehensive on seeing her so lively. With so much time on her hands, watching Vera so closely made her feel as though the tiny baby were an extension of herself. The world between the four walls of the room was large enough for her. The white walls appeared luxurious behind fading prints of landscapes even though the paint was cracking, even when the occasional gap painted over in white could not hide the deteriorating masonry. Alina did not mind that the wooden floor creaked nor that the bed would sink in the middle a little bit more each night. Neither was she bothered by the starkness of the cold light from the neon lamp. The love she felt for Vera rose above the austerity of the place. For the first time she was enjoying her own life.

The money she had been given by the men clad in white coats was a small fortune compared to what her mother's husband paid her for ten hours of hard labour each day on the farm. Alina kept the roll of money inside a little sewing box given to her by her father on her eleventh birthday, weeks before he died. The accident on the farm had changed everything. She was determined to give Vera a better life.

She asked the young man at reception to help her write

a brief message to the old lady giving details of where she was staying. People in the city behaved with a generosity she had not known before. The young man's simple gesture of slipping her message into a white envelope surprised and confused her. Alina was not sure whether she should pay him for it. She thought it best to keep quiet and go along with it. She checked several times that the house number was the same as the one on the scrunched up scrap of paper the foreman had given her. Later she made sure that the number on the front of the house was the same as the one on the envelope. The young man had confirmed that it was close by. Just a few blocks away. She pushed the envelope through the letterbox and then went shopping with Vera strapped behind her. Her euphoria was restrained only by feeling the imprint of years of oppression she was leaving behind. Alina almost felt mischievous buying soap, oil and baby ointment, choosing products in the supermarket without worrying about the price. A cot and the luxury of a bath to avoid having to use the hostel's communal bathroom. Her silent shyness barely hid her excitement on laying out all the products on the bed like an unexpected bounty. With Vera on her back she seemed to glide back and forth carrying jugs of hot water from the bathroom to mix with the freezing cold water of the tap in their room. She rubbed her hands with the foamy soap. She had never smelt such a delicate perfume. Alina enjoyed the daily bath just as much as Vera did, chatting continually to her baby. Her new life with Vera was meaningful and made it easy to forget. She had adapted wholeheartedly to so much happiness.

The little television remained unplugged on a high shelf in a corner of the room. As the days passed by so did the danger now that Vera had her new rubber helmet protecting her. At night Alina would hear people coming and going in the street. Sometimes she sat in front of the window to watch them wander past in the distance. Sometimes she exchanged a few words with the neighbour who worked all day and went to bed early to take her little boy to school before going to work. When he came home from school in the afternoon the boy would visit Vera. He would touch the ball on her head and smile at her before running off to have his tea and play outside with the new ball.

At night the city felt lonely in her room just as at the farm where the television, which used to be in the living room, had ended up in her mother's bedroom, after her father had died and the new husband had moved in. They would eat in the kitchen in silence, the man devouring his food like a voracious animal. Her mother would get up from the table every so often to clear the kitchen. The man would send Alina to bed after supper. From her room she would hear her mother laughing with her new man. Those few minutes before collapsing exhausted into bed were devastatingly lonely. Having to share her precious moments of leisure with the couple was abhorrent to her. Not that she had many such moments. She avoided them. Apart from the enforced minutes in the kitchen at supper each day, her time was spent putting up with the man's peremptory orders or her mother's indifference.

Alina had never had a television in her own room. Although an unforeseen luxury, she ignored it for the first few days. When she eventually plugged it in it reminded her of her father. They would sit and watch cartoons at the end of the day's work. Life had changed so suddenly. If only her father could see how this violent man had taken his place and had imposed his will. He would have punched his lights out. She used to dream that her father returned to take back his home. She was also used to the fact that her dream would just remain precisely that: a dream.

Alina was one of many who would never have the opportunity to travel to the United States. For several days most of the news on her television came from America. The flag in the background was unmistakable. The images flashed intermittently across her face. She was soon aware that the cans of soft drink which had been circulating could have turned her into a mere statistic among the hundreds of thousands of people who were incinerated in America. Every night, and sometimes during the day, she would turn on the television. Later she would unplug it telling herself it was the last time. The next day Alina could not help herself. After leaving Vera asleep in her cot, washing up and making soup on the hob in her room -even when looking for something else to do, she ended up turning on the television. Time after time she took in the figures, the images, the consequences, the forecasts. Life in the rented room seemed not to offer her the kind of protection she had thought it would. She would gaze at Vera for a long while before going to bed, making sure she was breathing. Nobody was safe. Alina feared not only for her baby but also for herself. The thought of being unable to look after her baby brought a new kind of disquiet, a feeling that came back every time she watched TV. The horror could happen to anybody.

As Vera slept she witnessed the news panel guest adjusting his tie in between questions. No, he was not adjusting his tie. He was trying to loosen it. Trying to breathe. He soon began to twist and leant forward in front of the cameras. This was not the physical presence of stiff corpses in the wheat fields or the men in the truck. Those bodies were lifeless. It had for her the immediacy of the screen, seconds before the final moment. Inevitability, which opens life up to death through the fine line that separates them. An almost transparent veil which, when withdrawn, restores the nothingness which had preceded existence. The TV crew had not had time to react and cut the broadcast. The guest appeared to recover and sat upright. And there he remained. Staring riveted at the camera still fixed on him as if it were inquiring about the beyond.

The nurse had warned her that on the news they talked only of death. Alina had looked into that stare and could not get it out of her mind. She sought answers to questions she hardly knew existed. She would lose herself in her thoughts for increasingly longer periods of time. The world outside the room appeared distant but had touched her closely. Alina had been in the fields. She had lived in the flesh the initial awareness, being first to witness the obscene truth. She was haunted by recurring thoughts. Feelings of precariousness returned once more. Days spent alone in the room began to feel unfamiliar. Vera seemed like a different being, as if she were no longer a part of her, or of the reality of which she was unaware. A reality concentrated inside the small television and expanded throughout the room to be concentrated once again in her mind. So densely that she thought her head would explode.

When she thought the worst was happening in the USA, reports soon began to emerge of deaths in Israel, Russia, Italy, the United Kingdom, France. Other affected countries suffered isolated cases of only a few thousand. It would later become obvious to her that the hundreds of thousands of deaths in each country were just the tip of the iceberg. In these instances there were no direct attacks. The toxins arrived in the imported syrup for making soft drinks. In many cases routine water testing had been omitted from the manufacturing process. Spokespersons for the soft drinks companies were interviewed on television. Explanations were hazy. They said that expert analysts would not have been able to identify the presence of such a complex agent. In defence of their companies they claimed that quality controls had been performed as well as regular bacteriological testing. Several top executives did not make it, whether by contagion or at their own hands was left unsaid. Soft drink factories were closed down by court order. Weeks later the only talk was of the possible death of the entire defenceless worldwide population, arbitrarily under the sun or the moon. The same moon which had witnessed Vera's birth on the Day of Judgment.

When Vera was old enough to understand what had happened the day she was born, the cataclysm was no longer mentioned. Some sort of taboo had emerged from the deep-seated fear within those who remembered the events and the feeling of unease of those who, like Vera, had been born since. Once the last corpse had been incinerated, a tacit silence reigned among the population, like a final seal that put paid to the horror.

Alina had all but given up on ever receiving the call when the young man from reception gave her the message. It felt like she had been living in the rented room for months, not weeks. She was worried that the money would run out. She had bought a few expensive items. The sewing box seemed larger every time she opened it. She spent hours stacking coins, counting the days, doing sums and apologising to Vera. She would take out the rolled-up bills and show them to her.

'For our food. We're going to a much better place. They'll call us soon. We must protect ourselves. I don't want you seeing horrible things like I did.'

At night Alina would remove the rubber helmet and put the cot near the window where Vera would be bathed in moonlight.

She asked the young man at reception to read the message to her twice. She had barely understood it the first time in anticipation of the news.

'I told you we'd be going somewhere nicer. To that big house I showed you. Mummy's going to work.'

Alina bought two large bags of sweets and gave one to the boy with the ball and the other to the young man at reception, who was disappointed that it was not a bottle of wine. On leaving the room for the last time Alina slammed the door, telling herself she wanted nothing further to do with television or with death.

She had never been in a town house before. The front of the house gave no real idea of its true size. When they arrived the old lady took them to their room. She showed her the whole house and the places where everything lived. Her husband had been the one who took care of it all.

'He looked after me as though I were made of glass', she said, hoping Alina would do the same now that he was gone.

She was glad it was a large house. She began working even harder than she used to on her mother's farm. Alina needed to fill her time. Even though she no longer knew whether she felt happy, she was less fearful for Vera. Everything seemed to be better, in spite of the small size of her room, the darkness and the overwhelming silence. At last Vera had the protection she needed. Alina had not been wrong. Nothing could happen to them in that old house with thick, high walls. With a job and a roof over their heads, life had become normal for her, who preferred not to know what was happening outside. Just like the old lady who could hardly hear and never left the house. Once she had given her instructions, the old lady scarcely spoke to her. She could barely talk at nearly ninety years old, she said. She did not speak because she preferred to live in the torpor of her memories. She would fall asleep in whichever armchair she was sitting in. In her dreams she was reunited with her husband and life became real for her. During the day she lived without him as if in a bad dream. She would walk the few steps from one armchair to the other and from there to the table and then to bed. The wait seemed endless. Her home had become a waiting room in which there was nothing to do until the moment of reunion. Inertia got her through the days as though she were not even there. After several days without speaking she would exchange a few phrases, to which Alina responded in monosyllables. It's better that way, thought the old lady. She did not realise that her maid's silence was so deeply ingrained that it had taken her to an unknown, dangerous place.

The day the last element of the synthetic substance was finally discovered, there was no stopping the brutal and irreversible decision to strike back.

The biological synthesis of two poisons and a bacteriological agent, a hybrid of three: botulinum, atropine and ricin, was the exterminating formula. The third element was the same as had been found in the Al-Qaeda caves in Afghanistan. Ricin prevents the formation of cell proteins. The size of a pinhead is enough to kill anyone in less than six hours leaving no trace evidence. Nobody claimed responsibility for the events. The silence was profound. The atrocity of the consequences inconceivable.

At the convent, Benedita was the only one who read the news in the Bari *Leggo*. Her friend Dugati, who worked for the newspaper would send it to her three times a week. This time the perpetrators would have nothing to celebrate, he assured her. The suspicions being aired in the press were not unfounded. Potential groups could be counted on the fingers of one hand: Al-Qaeda from the Algerian Sahara, Iraq, Pakistan, Afghanistan. In the arid and inhospitable regions of North Africa, beyond law and control. It could also be the GICM, responsible for the Madrid bombings or extremist factions of Hezbollah or the Jihadis, fundamentalist groups supported by the Taliban. To Benedita, the oxymoron in their names said it all: 'Groups for Prayer and Combat'. For Dugati conjectures served no purpose. Circumstances had not changed. It began with the recruitment of young people with no future. Lost inside their own heads, he reflected. Unfathomable young men like wild dogs in search of a bone to gnaw, jumping from one rubbish tip to another. Until they find their purpose, their daily bread. Some younger than fifteen years old would find the only light that crossed their path: the one that fanned the flames of hate. It was difficult for Benedita to conceive of this. The process was not elaborate. They could find all they needed to know in the training videos and coded forums on the internet. Trips would follow to Iran, Syria, Lebanon, Pakistan, the Maghreb countries. Training cells which operated from trucks constantly on the move. Led by good organisers, reliant on income from cocaine trafficking. All sponsored by the marriage of convenience to the Tuareg for the smuggling of chemicals.

'You don't need to be an expert,' Dugati told her, 'to see what sparks it off. Unemployment does not tally with the thousands of millions of dollars spewed out by oil. Lack of opportunities leads to one or the other. A belt loaded with explosives or a lifebelt to cross the Mediterranean to a better life.'

Before the cataclysm, Benedita would visit the newspaper offices, next to the bank where she would cash the cheque the diocese sent to the community every month.

Mother Teresa knew nothing about Benedita's meetings with her friend Dugati. There was nothing sinful in them, although their content did stray from the pious life. She and Dugati would have infrequent but lively chats.

'If I weren't a nun, I'd be a journalist, Dugati,' she joked with her friend, who smiled, flattered. 'If it weren't for you, I would know nothing about the outside world.'

Countless times they had talked about the crisis. Both suspected that sooner or later the financial debacle would be a thermometer for the impending fireball which was approaching at a blistering speed.

'They don't seem to want to admit it, sister. Laboratories the world over keep investing in innovation, while carbon emissions grow as high as the resulting GDP. They don't see the severity of higher temperatures but they will see the consequences. On top of that, there's the food crisis and the millions depending on food aid! The UN has recently stopped delivering due to petrol shortages, so the hungry are furiously taking to the streets in sub-Saharan Africa, Senegal, Indonesia and India. Soya is just benefiting a few while the production of biofuels is triggering rises in the price of basic foodstuffs.'

Some of the information Benedita would absorb with keen interest. The rest filled her with anxiety.

'Sister, do you know why African children are not going to school? Hunger prevents them getting up from their beds or separating from their mothers' arms. Sometimes their mothers take them to die in hospital, where they also have no food to offer them. A billion people with diseases from starvation.'

Benedita would sometimes question what she was doing at the convent apart from praying.

"I'm going to give a fund-raising talk a week tomorrow at 7 pm,' Dugati said, handing her a leaflet. 'Can you come? Who knows, you can help me collect contributions in the chapel on Sundays."

'I'm so sorry I can't attend. It would not be possible for me to leave the convent in the evenings.'

'Don't worry, sister.'

'I would still like to hear what you have to say. Will you be able to print it out for me?'

'You might be shocked. It's a different world.'

'I know and I think we should all know.'

That was the world in which Vera had been growing in her mother's womb. The world into which she arrived was to be very different although it appeared to be the same. Alina had not known that reality either, even though her own was tragic. On the farm the only news of any interest had been limited to its own small perimeter. At best, it could include the village. There was no time to understand how people lived elsewhere. From six o'clock in the morning, or five in summer, there was a string of tasks to be performed in the fields, barns, pens and stores. Followed by the tasks which awaited inside the house until nightfall. There everything was palpable, undeniable. Life there demanded minute-by-minute attention. Outside that perimeter the rest belonged to an unknown and almost inexistent universe.

Dugati's fund-raising presentation just days before the cataclysm now seemed outdated and absurd to Benedita a few weeks later. As if time had speeded up to make whole universes disappear in a flash.

Sitting in her cloister room, Benedita re-read Dugati's lecture: 'Ladies and gentlemen, I will be brief. You will be aware by now of the aim of this meeting. Allow me a few minutes of your time. The financial debacle has forced the G8 to create a package of global measures to avoid total collapse. China and Russia, with trillions in reserves in foreign currencies, have extended a helping hand to western banks.

There is hope that values could change or that something could be done about the lack of them. Some believe that the American neocon clique is about to be knocked down at the feet of a reality it ignores. I think they are optimists. I believe that war is still their priority. They will not reform markets to share them more equitably. If they do they would risk losing control of resources and markets. For them fear of freefall would justify all actions. Renewed investment in the economy of war could save the energy project and the shrinking markets. With a deficit of hundreds of billions they cannot afford to stop the machinery. The new face in the White House has once again fallen into the void. Interests and ideology are inseparable. Invasions on foreign soil never include a real commitment to civilian services or the needs of citizens. The world knows that and allows it to continue. They are condemned by one discourse and justified by another. Neither approved nor censured. Merely silenced. We are sitting on a time bomb. Now we also have earthquakes, floods, tsunamis, hurricanes, droughts, forest fires and the depletion of sources of fresh water. The excesses of a few and the hunger of many have set up camp both in democracies and in dictatorships. At the service of the US government and its crusades. Supporting oppressive dictatorships, the sale of arms to corrupt governments, secret machinations, undercover diplomacy. With the media by their side every inch of the way, moulding opinion. Legitimising interventionism. Precepts like advertising slogans to sell arms, politics, business, oil, war.'

To her it seemed devastating. It was a different world, just as he had said. She felt the urge to escape. Not from Dugati's words, but from the precise time when there was no turning back from the present.

For Benedita the thought of the world being able to renew the established order looked quite impossible. However, there was a change. The least expected though the most drastic. Not by the action of politicians, nor by government measures, or the collaboration of NGOs. It was not thanks to religions, nor lobbying by human rights committees. The change was neither gradual nor planned. It happened overnight. It was the end for a world which had long been clamouring for a new outlook. It had arrived. It was not the caring approach that it clamoured for, nor the merciful awareness it hoped for. It was a cold and inevitable stance which demanded full and unconditional attention. That demanded by terror. The most atrocious act, dexterous in its capacity for destruction without damage to the integrity of any of mankind's creations. Destruction only aimed at human lives.

What was happening was not alien to the old lady. She had known one war. This one was not how she suspected it to be nor one her late husband could ever have imagined. Her dearly departed husband had had to fight. He had been on the front line. She kept his medals together with his gold tooth and a bullet. The old lady knew about the subdued pride her beloved had felt for having taken part in such a just cause. The honour of serving. He would regale her with stories about how his platoon had conquered the hill, how they bravely ran on in spite of the burst of machine-gun fire. How the courageous platoon of fourteen had managed to take the bunker and capture the sniper in the trench. He had received his medal despite falling as part of the advance party. He had taken a bullet in the right buttock. He also regretted having been the only one to be decorated. While he was recovering, the platoon had again gone into action. The group of thirteen had been felled by a landmine. An ambush immediately afterwards had left them with no chance to defend themselves. They were left lying in the woods, their bodies abandoned with no hope of a decent burial. The old lady patiently reassured him that he had nothing to blame himself for. Every so often she would console him. His memories confused him as the order of events turned against him to make him feel responsible. He had only been as brave as his fellow soldiers. He had not withdrawn. How could he be at the front of the platoon if he could barely walk? She avoided using the word 'luck'. She smiled to herself, grateful for the bullet which had saved his life. She could not tell her courageous captain that she felt nothing for the death of his soldiers. The only thing she cared about was that he had come back alive. She silently preferred love to honour. In the house where they had been so happy, all that now remained were these few souvenirs which the old lady took out of the ebony box and placed on the bed every Sunday. One by one she would take out the medals, letters, photos of his fellow soldiers. She would polish the bullet between her fingers, remembering the warmth of his skin. She would then leave it on the pillow where he no longer laid his head next to hers. Slowed down by the years, she re-read each of his seven letters. The only ones she had ever received from her husband during the only weeks in which life had separated them. They were expressions of love and honour. He did not want to upset her with the practical aspects of war. With her he used words nobody used on the front, in the trenches, or in hospitals, not even in the barracks. There the language used was that of reality. His letters were the artifice which brought some hope to the old lady. The honour of war and the words associated with it had resonated throughout so many stories. History nurtured the myth of the values of war by repeating its favoured terms: honour, heroic, victory. They tainted everyday life. Even the old lady's wrinkled hands on the white linen sheets. There she rested the objects, an expression of honour. As played out from one century to the next, the old lady latched on to the same words she had heard on the lips of her beloved. Now the new generations had their opportunity. To start all over again. That was it. It was not clear to her where the danger came from this time. No matter. As she recalled him saying, we have to save the world.

'Haven't you heard about the war?' the old lady asked Alina looking at her, eyes wide open, awaiting an answer, which did not come.

'They call it the Third World War. But it is all happening in countries on the other side. It won't affect us. Here nothing will harm us as long as we don't have any soft drinks.'

Alina did not understand any of this. She could only perceive the danger and the need to protect Vera. The rest was a nightmare she had to overcome. Like the nightmare which had begun on the farm following her eleventh birthday and her father's accident. She waited in vain for his return from hospital. She had seen him work tirelessly. With very little, he had rebuilt a ruined smallholding, turning it into a small treasure he looked after as if it were a grand estate. He had managed to afford the luxury of hiring a labourer for a couple of days a week. His dream had ended in misfortune. Just when life had begun to improve for the three of them, he had had the accident. Her father would not sit again in front of the brand new television. The labourer took to wearing his shoes. A few days later, his death. At her age she thought this only happened to animals, insects or plants. She carried on at school as if nothing had happened. Her mother had not even felt the need to let her know. As if that morning's event had been banal, as if it was not worthy of her immediate presence. When Alina got home from school that afternoon her father was already in a box. The electricity which ran through her body drove her little hands. She wanted to open it even if she lost her fingernails. The box was sealed. She was not allowed to see him. The perplexing explanations, the adults' meaningless words had dried her tears. Her mother barely put her hand on her shoulder while the labourer talked with some men in the kitchen, who later carried out the box and heaved it up onto the back of his own pickup. If she was going to wake up from that dream, that would have been the moment to do so. It had all been so quick. The priest was waiting for them at the cemetery standing beside next to the gravedigger. Apart from him, nobody said anything. The three of them sitting in the pickup cab – she herself, her mother and the labourer. Behind them her father leaving this life also unable to say a word.

From then on there was no more school. The new circumstances made themselves felt immediately. As dark a transformation as it was violent. A few days were enough to make it clear that the labourer was there to stay. It was explained to her in few words. He had helped her mother deal with her father's death. Not only would he stay to carry on working, he would head the farm. He would take charge of everything, working hard to give them both a future. They had not said anything to her, but now the labourer also went into her parents' bedroom. At night from her bed, Alina would wait until sleep won her over, listening out for the bedroom door which would not open again until the next morning. A few weeks later the priest's visit surprised them all. It confirmed what she had not dared to imagine. 'I'm glad you've decided to stay to look after them. From what I understand, I think you should marry.' He said to the couple with a stern look. The labourer could not have predicted a better outcome. It was then that Alina cried for her father. Bitterly on the day of her mother's wedding to the labourer. It was a Sunday on the way to the livestock market. She was the only witness. It was not a social event. Nothing that happened on the farm involved the community. It all took place behind closed doors.

The new husband had decided that the girl should help them on the farm. This was no time to be studying. The bank was not granting loans and her father had left nothing but debts. That was one of the explanations which seemed totally incomprehensible to Alina. The brusque transformation took her unawares. She had led a simple but good life before the danger. She knew life could be gentle and sweet. She had experienced such moments with her father. As time passed, the violence that the new husband began to inflict upon them made no sense to her. Nor would the deaths on television later on.

Saving the world. Conspiracy theorists were shouting from the rooftops that, in their final attempt at oppression, the neocons had provided weapons against their own security to enable them later on to save the world. Theories were recycled. A state of siege was declared and the army took over.

People around the world and their governments were too weakened by the cataclysm to offer any strong opposition. Retaliation was neither approved nor condemned by the international community. The silence was even greater than the horror. The terrorist attack had been virtually unilateral, as had its consequences. That was reason enough for the superpower's counterattack, which hailed from the cowboy era: wild Indians against armies in defence of justice. Except that losses now were vastly more costly in terms of human lives and destruction. The flag of democracy had been left in tatters by the constant battering which preceded the cataclysm. These events, as though in a pressure cooker, were condensed before the explosion.

The world had divided unsustainably. The disaster movie had become part of life. A conclusion was expected. With everyone gripped on the edge of their seats in front of the screen, almost without breathing the denouement unfolded. Shiny missiles shot out in all directions. Against all Jeffersonian principles, the manoeuvre ensued in a burst of vengeance, almost unplanned. Justification tied on to missiles like messenger doves of death. With decades of preparation costing millions and ideals and guarantees of human progress. So similar it was like holding up a mirror to past empires justifying their claims of civilization.

With self-proclaimed right, the US launched the most brutal attack in history. The Forty-Day War had started. Missiles fell in Iran, Iraq, Afghanistan and Pakistan. The confusion which reigned following the bioterrorist attack was equalled and surpassed by that of retaliation. The destruction made it impossible to tend to the injured, care for the displaced, distribute food. It was not only civil and military chaos. Governments of countries suffering the onslaught were disabled, giving way to another military force for a third assault. Retaliation by those who had suffered retaliation. This time against Israel. The counterattack on Israel brought out the disciples of the prophecies of destruction.

The convent closed its eyes to the horror. Father Zillo urged the community to pray night and day. Not only was it the only thing they could do, he would tell them, it was essential. Only Benedita interrupted her prayers to find out about the world. Mother Teresa understood that Father Zillo would not want to keep them up to date about the devastation.

"See, Sister, read this piece,' Dugati invited Benedita to sit by his side while he searched for a document in his laptop. 'I don't think it goes against your beliefs. The way things are, I don't think it's just coincidence. Have you heard of Nostradamus? Please read this paragraph. In his predictions he talks about the end of the world, the karmic mass and the prelude to the arrival of the Antichrist.' He handed her his laptop.

Benedita read the piece through to the end. The coincidences with recent events were staggering:

'National territorial operations under false pretexts and their culmination in the Third World War will lead to the extermination of practically the entire population. Eight bombs will explode in eight cities of the USA on the same day. Although incapable of recovery, big brother USA will counterattack with all its might against the Muslim world. China will supply arms to Muslim countries reduced to a mountain of rubble in six days, with hatred against the USA directed at Israel. Social turmoil and the weakening of political structures will promote the arrival of the Antichrist. The USA, at the mercy of a natural disaster, will be devastated as a nation, creating conflict, despair and destitution. In economic ruin, it will be hard put to deal with the disaster. Another three powerful nations will send help to assist its citizens. Changes will come about which will help the Antichrist take over the world and use populations like slaves.'

It was real events articulating the prophetic words. Benedita was not disturbed nor, as usual, did she share the predictions with the community. Even though at that point she could not explain why, she still had hope, she told Dugati. She had never felt so calm, as if she had a sense of the future. She was also very selective about what information she passed on to Mother Teresa. She had enough to do dealing with Sister Eulalia and her increasingly frequent panic attacks.

When governments had almost given up on finding a way out, the last report of the last death reached the news agencies. In a few months the terrorist pandemic and the war which followed had annihilated half the world population seven hundred years on from the Great Plague of the 14th century initiated on the steppes of Central Asia. This time it had begun in the city which was the symbol of economic power, the steppe of the capitalist world spreading throughout the territory like a lit fuse. The warmongering drive came to an end in a final death rattle of violence. Neighbours exchanged shocked looks as if they had never seen each other before. The events were kept in the silence of incredulity.

PART II

Darkness had seeped into her. She had remained bound to that instant which lay between life and death. Alina no longer watched television. Inexplicable as it was, she had understood everything. She needed to know no more. With no outlook for the future, her inner pace became attuned to the quiescence of the old lady and her daydreams. As she became familiar with the housework routines in the old lady's house, Alina began to adopt a leisurely rhythm which bore her along from chore to chore throughout the day until nightfall. Chores became routine. Some of them utterly unnecessary, a pointless repetition of the past. The ritual waxing of the floor, whose shine the old lady could barely discern. Polishing a few bits of silverware, briefly aired before being relegated once more to the darkest depths of the sideboard. Cleaning mirrors which no longer played host to any human reflection other than the drifting shadow of the old lady with her bowed head. The old house continued to be well looked after, regardless. Decades of routine resisting the futility of the present, in readiness each day, irrespective of any purpose. Perhaps awaiting the arrival of others or of a day when life would once again take over.

The things that kept Alina busy hardly affected her life or that of the old lady. She failed to notice the redundancy of her actions. She rarely went to Vera in her new static perception of time. The hours passed by slowly but surely, evolving into something closer to the essence of being. Vera would suckle at her mother's breast whenever they had contact, absorbing the few words her mother murmured to her from her new, mesmerising world.

The silence of the days was barely broken by Vera's occasional crying announcing that it was time for her feed. It was a sound that brought her mother to life like no other. It dispelled the half-darkness to reward her with few minutes of rapture a day. In a natural, close communion without reservation or aspiration; without artifice or conditions. As if under a brief spell, she would be infused with light emanating from Vera in spite of the surroundings. Free from the past, without future. Only the precise time of being. Save for those intervals of restorative feeding, day after day Vera went from the darkness of the day to the moonlit window at night.

The simplicity of the day-to-day routine brought the two women of otherwise disparate generations closer together. They shared an almost wordless understanding, sensing each other in the silence. They echoed each other more than either of them could grasp. Their apathy bound them closer than their obvious social standings separated them. The world was shut off from their daily contact.

Once a month the old lady went into the pantry with Alina. She would stand before the tins, bags and boxes of dried food. Each month she would say the same thing, without the slightest inflection in her voice. Like a script she had acted out too many times, made monotonous by the indifference of time.

'I can't see properly. What else do we need? We'll order only what we need. We aren't given to extravagance anymore.' Struggling to emerge briefly from her stupor, Alina would respond.

'Write it down, please.' The old lady would hand her the yellowed paper and the pencil she had sharpened unnecessarily before entering the pantry. With Alina by her side, dictating what she had written, only just intelligibly, the old lady placed the order for those depleted provisions. Once a fortnight they would open the door to receive a basket of fruit and vegetables which would soon also dry up or be consumed, just like the old lady and her maid. It was the only source of life entering the house where everything seemed to be motionless and unchanging save for the bluish light surrounding Vera in her cot.

Outside, the world continued to bustle. Surviving populations were relocated to make way for reconstruction, as urgent a task as it was painful. Life in those cities which had not suffered a direct hit gradually returned to normal over a few months. There was a palpable feeling of relief at the encouraging news. The convent celebrated with psalmodies the diluted version of the news that Benedita passed on from Dugati. The first world directive for a ceasefire and general amnesty was followed by the start of the sixty-day summit to reformulate a physically and morally ruined world. One by one, practical solutions for the new order were suggested, debated, approved and eventually adopted by consensus. The G20 spread their arms to become the G35, welcoming developing countries that were rich in oil and reserves. China, India, Brazil, Indonesia, Russia, Saudi Arabia. The G35 and representatives of UN Member States met while the stench of death was still rising to the sky like a rancid prayer. This time the world that had plodded on with no sense of urgency had been shaken by its own reality. The new world order had decided to stop looking the other way. Step by step a natural balance took over to alter the weights on the scales. The world that emerged from the destruction was being remade.

Once normal banking activity had been resumed, Father Zillo no longer went to the convent with their monthly allowance. The Vatican needed him more than ever to operate within the new economic structure in order to survive. Invited as the Vatican's financial representative, Zillo took part in hearings and round tables, within think tanks summoned to work towards establishing a world at peace.

'I have some important news to read to you, my dear Mother.' Over the phone, he read out an excerpt from the universal decree to Mother Teresa. 'From now on the world will count on each and every survivor, it will no longer be possible to survive without genuine cooperation. Governments are to have a level playing field. Many have not played a role in the past. The world will now be able to settle that debt.' Nations have finally voted to establish foundations for a new society and it was unanimous.'

The world was barely able to hold itself together when, in an unprecedented summit, the new G35 and the UN General Assembly drafted a world constitution which would prevent new threats. Just as in 1945, world leaders were queuing up to sign a peace agreement. Once the summit was over, the UN took political control of the world. The World Government was born.

America had no choice but to abide by the latest rules of the new order. The rekindled international mistrust in the superpower compounded the devastation of its farming infrastructure, with land ending up not only unproductive, but toxic. Now that time was not measured in incinerations, cleanups, health controls, safety and aid for the population, procedures were traced and details of the cataclysm came to light. Purging or absorption of the pathogens would take years, or longer. The US countryside would be a noxious cauldron for generations to come.

America depended on this new world to put their infected soil to another use. Most of the land was assigned to the generation of solar and wind power. Their operations in distant lands sought new ways to generate revenue. A new attempt at rising from the ashes. The US made commendable efforts to overcome disaster. Like a vast wasteland, its barren land and its landscape were covered in wind turbines and solar panels. The American countryside was slowly becoming one huge power plant, its skin covered in silver scales and long white splinters rising to the blue sky, as if the only thing alive were the air. Extensive wind farms buzzing constantly were a sign of danger to all forms of life tempted to approach the ground where only metallic spikes could survive. Paper-thin rolls of solar material were printed in Germany like newspapers. Giant solar power plants with huge mirrors extracted what the northern soil could not provide in a forgotten world where five billion had lived with no energy. Now thermal storage systems not only ensured abundance in the supply of energy but the second coming of the growth boom. More significant was the second coming of Latin America. Reinstated as the granary of the world it now made up for the systemic barrenness of its northerly neighbours by exporting round the clock. Brazil, with its endless reserves of fresh water in its innumerable rivers, became a saviour of the thirsty North by exporting clean water used for drinking, food preparation and supplying the various industries that now kept it afloat.

The structure of global labour and production adapted tamely to the drastic changes in the world after the cataclysm and the Third World War. It was decided at the summit that foodstuffs and agricultural products should be produced locally where the earth was fertile and water had not been contaminated.

The new G35 injected money into the markets and banks, with the creation of a new world authority for financial and banking control to guarantee stability. Measures were applied globally to end trade wars which had already begun. After the removal of protectionism, thirty seven tax havens were eliminated and with them money laundering and the mafias.

With investment by emerging Asian economies buying companies, merging with fallen countries from the old First World, a single world economy took shape. Shared interests enabled alliances to be forged. Suddenly all the proposals, excuses, alibis were removed like an iron curtain that had proved impossible to raise under the weight of individual interests.

What happened beyond the frontiers of the house was alien to Alina and the old woman. It was as if they had started out on a self-absorbing, lethargic race with death as the finishing line. When Alina stopped eating, the old lady also failed to notice that the daily chores were often left undone. The intervals between stocking the pantry became increasingly longer. Fresh food would spoil before the old lady, with her weak appetite, had got around to consuming it. Almost without knowing where the day began or ended, the hours of sleep would lengthen to shorten time. In the darkness of the house, the old lady's tired eyes did not see the dust gathering nor the cobwebs dangling across the corners awaiting the denouement. One by one the usual household noises faded away. Alina's toing and froing, the ticking of the grandfather clock in the dining room. The old lady no longer missed the chimes which in another era she had anticipated with an aficionado's zeal. She barely heard Vera's inconsolable crying as she clamoured in vain to be fed.

That morning as usual, the old lady, who could only just manage to shuffle from room to room, rang the bell she used instead of her voice. The minutes stretched on as she waited just like the increasingly loud grating sound that came from Vera's vocal chords, now clamouring for dear life. There was nothing that might be holding up her maid except the vital duty of feeding her baby. Why was the child crying if she was with her mother? If she had been ill, she would have told her. Alina had never gone out without telling her and it was simply impossible that Alina could not hear the piercing sound of the bell. She rang it at intervals almost certain that her maid would not come. If she did not answer Vera's bawling, it was even less likely she would answer the bell let alone the cracked, weakened voice of an old lady. The routine and peace which were her only consolation were disrupted. With the passing of the hours and the fixed attention the old lady directed for the first time to Vera's rhythmic crying, a forgotten feeling began to take hold. A shift away from the emotional paucity that had settled over her life – an event barely reflected in her eyes. It was expressed by her hands through the sound of alarm she had initiated. With each ring she felt unfettered concern taking root. The instinctive, primal response which was reborn in spite of her wrinkles. The protective instinct which despite herself revived what seemed barren. Little by little her indifference was transformed like the inside of a magician's hat revealing a symbolic white dove. It was the child who asked her. The transformation was complete. As though on a high-level mission, the old lady, not without effort, ventured to the room at the back passing through the drawing room, dining room, kitchen and pantry. She had hardly any strength left when she poked her head in before entering. The scene was unequivocal. She had almost sensed it beforehand. At last with a superhuman impulse she lifted up the crying baby and removed her from the room like a fireman saving the last victim of a fire. The old lady who was already so much closer to death did not need to approach the bed to check whether Alina was breathing or touch her skin to understand. Without much thought, with an intuition that came from years of a spiritual bond with her deceased loved one, the old woman understood Alina's death to have a bigger significance than the circumstances surrounding it. The implications would be revealed at the right time.

The afternoon prior to Alina's death, Vera had let her mother know that the two hemispheres of her brain had already closed up. Several little slaps on the rubber helmet had been enough. So Alina had removed the cap and placed it on the altar. Like a bell, covering the Polaroid of her smiling with her hand on the belly which had protected Vera for nine months. She had no idea how long she sat beside the cot. By evening only the darkness had come in through the window. She sought the moon where she knew it would be.

'Where's your moon, Vera? The moon's gone. Let's go and find it.' Alina picked Vera up in her arms. Standing next to the window, Vera, with her bare head smiling, while her mother showed her the stars in the black, moonless sky. That night the stars made up for its absence. When she had given birth there had been a diaphanous full moon. Now the waning moon had completed its cycle. When it began the next one Vera would no longer have her mother by her side. Alina fed her baby until she was satisfied in the darkness of the starry sky. She gazed at her for hours under the street lamp. She wanted to seal the image in her pupils and take it with her in her final sleep. She had kissed her on her forehead before lying down next to the cot. Nine months on from Vera's birth, Alina never got up again.

As if by a miracle, a long-forgotten droplet rolled down from the old lady's red eyes into the furrows of her cheek while she stroked the baby girl's translucent skin with her dry fingers and waited for Sister Benedita. When the old lady had called the convent, the nun had no hesitation. She agreed to take the child, even without having consulted her community. Benedita was well aware of convent rules and the clause on abandoned children. Technically speaking Vera had been abandoned by her mother. They could not deny her authorisation to take charge of the baby until she was adopted.

Vera arrived at the convent with pallid skin and huge eyes. In spite of their reservations the nuns passed her from arm to arm in a game she took to with glee. The more she was passed around the more she laughed and kicked in excitement, as if her energy grew in each restorative embrace. She ate her food with an inspiring appetite. There was nothing she did not like and nothing that Benedita did not give her for the sheer pleasure of seeing her grow. She was no longer pallid and her eyes shone healthily. Benedita had seen that light.

'Are you sure it won't interfere?'

'I promise, Reverend Mother.'

'We rely on the vegetable garden.'

'You won't notice any difference.'

'Most of them object. And those who don't, well, you know, it's as if they did. If you want to look after the child, you'll have to do so on your own.'

'Yes, Reverend Mother.'

She had thought it through. There were only two problems to solve; she needed a pram and a high chair. She called the newspaper to place the usual advertisement during the months of shortages, when the diocese was forced to skip some of the monthly payments. Readers were familiar with the heading 'Request for donation to the convent'. When Dugati first suggested the idea, Benedita could not refuse. Months later it had become the normal thing to do. While she waited, she did what she knew best: she improvised. Every morning she wrapped Vera in a blanket and took her to the vegetable garden in the wheelbarrow she used to transport plants and tools. She would put her under a tree if it was too sunny. If it rained, Benedita would entrench Vera on the bunk between her pillow and a couple of old habits while she worked on the convent's accounts on the computer which had also been donated. All she had to do was call Dugati for him to place an advertisement for free. She had convinced the Mother Superior that they should keep up with the times. By hand the accounts took days, with an accounting program, she explained to her, it was like putting coins in a slot machine. The machine made the calculations directly. She knew it was not the best analogy but could think of no other. The strictest nuns looked aghast at one another and then glared at the Mother Superior. Not all the sisters agreed with her methods. They abhorred publicity now that the convent had returned to normal monastic life, leaving behind the scandal of past decades. Every time disapproval surfaced Mother Teresa reminded those most prone to scolding that Benedita was the youngest, that her intentions were always pious and the results satisfactory.

For the first week of Vera's arrival, the Mother Superior had excused her from prayers in the chapel while she adapted to the new circumstances. When donations came the following week, Benedita did not think that resuming morning and two evening prayers in the chapel would be an even greater problem. She sat in the last seat at the back near the exit. She would leave Vera in her pram in the corridor where the baby could be heard. Although Vera only cried if she was hungry, the refusal to allow her to be present during prayers was categorical. The annoyed looks of some of the sisters who insisted on sitting near the altar as usual, leaving her isolated at the back, convinced her that she had to settle all differences. It had taken a huge effort to get them to accept Vera in the dining hall, even during vows of silence, three days a week. She prayed each night next to Vera's cot for the sisters to open their hearts just as she had done. Although it seemed to her that the atmosphere improved bit by bit, the third advertisement asking for a donation to the convent was too much for Sister Eulalia.

'Reverend Mother, how far are these adverts going to go? Next time it will be a television to distract her or a washing machine to cope with the nappies…'

'I'll have a word with the sister.'

'Donations have always been voluntary. What will people think? That we're taking advantage of the war.'

'I hear you. I'll talk to her.'

'We don't want any more scandals in this house…'

'Do I have to tell you again?'

'Forgive me, Reverend Mother.'

The baby monitor was the answer. Benedita prepared sweet potato purée, which Vera loved so that her stomach would be full before leaving for the chapel. She would leave her sleeping in the sacristy. From there the little sounds she made while asleep -and which provoked hidden giggles among the prayers- were amplified. Benedita never imagined that in those moments in which the monitor was on, the sisters were taking it in turns to check that Vera was all right. Sometimes they even took her a piece of bread or a biscuit to suck on. In time the little signs left among the blankets or on the floor showed just how far she could push the limits within the community. Weeks went by without Benedita preparing the adoption advertisement. The interval between her confessions became a cause for alarm. The presence of the baby girl had drawn more attention than ever to her eccentric behaviour. She had managed to make herself busy during the two hours the confessor had available each week. Never before had she accumulated so many sins of omission. Father Tito, who came each Sunday to say mass and take the nuns' confessions, had no choice but to send her a message through the Mother Superior. He had already imagined, on seeing Benedita kneel down in the confessional, that it all had to do with the baby. Benedita did not mind about the penance as long as the little lies she would tell Mother Teresa were limited to the priest's ears as a confessional secret. This time Sister Eulalia knowingly contradicted herself when she suggested to the Mother Superior that Benedita should speak to her friend at the newspaper. Placing the advert to find a new home for Vera could no longer be postponed.

'Benedita, you either place the notification and begin interviewing couples as we had agreed, or I will call the adoption agency.'

'Right away, Reverend Mother. My friend has been sick. If you don't mind my calling him next week…'

'Give me his name and I'll call him myself.'

'I'll do it now, Reverend Mother, I'll call him without delay.' With her head bowed Benedita acknowledged that she should not cross that limit.

Although the couples who began to arrive left delighted with Vera, many gave up in the face of an overwhelmingly long and complicated questionnaire with some very strange clauses. Benedita was also unable to find a suitable home among those couples who presented meticulously completed questionnaires. She knew Vera inside out. The home chosen had to be as special as the baby. Months went by and couples interested in adopting her came at increasingly longer intervals.

'Benedita, don't you think this questionnaire is a little overly elaborate?'

'Reverend Mother, with all due respect... You surely realise that Vera is not like any other child. Only a special couple could understand her.'

Benedita was familiar with the altruistic desire of so many couples to adopt children orphaned by the cataclysm and by war.

'Vera is the easiest child to look after that I have ever come across.'

'Reverend Mother, with all due respect... How many babies have you seen in this convent?'

By the time Vera was two years old, it was no longer a matter of Benedita's exclusive affection for the little girl. The other sisters also began to boycott interviews with applicant couples. Eventually the notification disappeared from the chapel anteroom. It was by chance that Mother Teresa found it with the day's crumbs among Vera's blankets minutes before public mass on Sunday.

'Reverend Mother, you know I've never lied to you... Reverend Mother, this time... I can assure you it wasn't me!', Benedita's categorical tone and the absence of respect in it were reason enough not only for the Mother Superior to believe her, but also for her to see that the sisters no longer held an objection to Vera staying.

Every Sunday the ritual of returning the notification to the notice board after general mass was repeated. Without any further exchanges with Mother Teresa, Benedita knew she could call Dugati so that he stopped publishing the announcement. Even though couples no longer came and

Benedita no longer printed requests and questionnaires, it was an implicit tradition that on Vera's birthday each year the Mother Superior asked the same question.

'Sister Benedita, where is the notification for Vera's adoption?'

Benedita would pull out from the pocket of her habit the yellowed paper folded in four. The Mother Superior would again put it up on the board with pins until the following Sunday.

Vera was already learning to walk. Benedita could hardly refuse when it was insisted that she and the girl should move to the room next to the unused parlour. On the ground floor they would be more independent and Vera would not be subjected to the unfortunate habits that the nuns had acquired over time. To Benedita the spacious drawing room with vast windows onto the garden and white shutters seemed like a luxury. Once she had cleaned up the windows, their bunks were lost on the now shimmering parquet. Mixing kerosene and used candle wax, Benedita had polished the floor beyond recognition. She hardly dared confess it to Sister Leopoldina, who giggled and forbade her from telling Sister Eulalia. Benedita would not let her come into her new polished room for fear that it would seem insolent that the candles that had once been burned in worship, plea or penance had ended up on the floor. At night, each in their bed, Benedita could hardly get to sleep as she surveyed it all. Although the new room was almost empty, she could not stop admiring the space. Buzzing with contentment, she was the happiest nun in the world. She felt blessed like no other, especially as she contemplated Vera sleeping soundly and safe. Vera, whom from a young age Benedita had sat in front of the computer, soon became a regular user. Firstly with games that entertained her, later on to do the homework her mentor would prepare for her. She would look into Benedita's spreadsheet showing her contemplative duties, mealtimes, meetings, chores, so that she could exchange a few words or laughs from their room over the baby monitor.

Days before Vera's fifth birthday Benedita felt anxious. People's resilience during the following years of conciliation and reconstruction, the results of which were beginning to be seen on streets all over the world, filled her with an overriding anxiety. It was true that the community had been blessed to the point that destruction had not visited them in the flesh; nor had the prophecies Dugati had told her about resulted in the predicted end of the world. She was concerned about the dramatic changes occurring in a world of which Vera would soon be a part. She wanted to ensure Vera's well-being within the walls of the convent. Above all, she wanted to preserve Vera from an unworthy universe. For no reason, she felt the need to have Vera's permanence officially confirmed. This was her place. At the same time she was apprehensive about seeking a direct answer from Mother Superior to her wish of bringing up Vera at the convent.

She had no option but to use a dishonest and unspeakable strategy.

It was not her intention to make Vera cry, although she knew it would happen inevitably when she revealed to Vera that the Mother Superior had intended to have her adopted.

'Darling, none of us want it but the only one who can decide is Mother Teresa,' she had said knowing that once Vera was aware all doubts would be dispelled.

The Mother Superior had already experienced personally Vera's exceptional nature. Conversations with her, though brief and intense, revealed the girl's lucidity. She was also amused by the foibles Vera had acquired from her mentor. There was a knock on the door. Mother Teresa was amused rather than surprised that it was Vera who had come along to ask for an audience. She gathered it would be either something extremely serious or just peculiar. Vera had never entered her office alone. Neither did she show any sign of consternation or shyness. Indeed, she had a self-assuredness about her that Mother Teresa had never seen among the congregation.

'Reverend Mother, with all due respect, I can read what it says on this paper.' With no need to approach Vera's extended hand, the Mother Superior recognised the notification which had been knocking around the convent for years.

'Who gave you that paper, Vera?'

'Nobody… No… It was on the floor.'

'Let me explain something to you…' the Mother Superior set about dealing with what seemed to her a challenge, but was cut short.

'Reverend Mother… with all due respect… My family is here. I don't want to go and live with anyone else.'

The insolent interruption and Vera's tight arms clasping her thighs as she buried her head in her lap left Mother Teresa unable to reply or explain. Vera's crying sealed the silence which became official on her fifth birthday. The Mother Superior never again asked about the notification and life carried on as usual. There was only one condition to which Benedita could not object.

A few months later Vera began attending the technical school a few blocks from the convent. Even though Benedita wanted to school her at home and had a syllabus outlined, she did recognise that the world outside was undergoing changes remarkably fast. However familiar she was with contemporary life, more so than the sisters, who were enclosed in their own bubble. Vera would be better off at school. At the suggestion of the Mother Superior, Benedita made an effort to smooth the difficult path of school life for the new student. The initial enthusiasm Benedita had passed on to Vera did not prevent Vera from feeling constrained for the first few weeks. It was a different world, open and noisy. She found the busy space much more restrictive than the cloister, where the silence let her listen to other sounds.

When Vera could not respond to the racket she withdrew into her own inner space. Her deep, measured breathing, which began on closing her eyes or staring into space took her to the same place she had known when from the sacristy she could hear the prayers repeated like a mantra. The litanies that were taught led her to a place unknown to the nuns which was beyond any prayer or mystery.

Now that Vera spent all day outside the community, Benedita alone in her room missed the routine. She was hoping that at any moment Vera would whisper a question to her by bringing the baby monitor closer to her mouth. She performed her duties with more determination than ever; the vegetables from the garden had never grown as big or been so plentiful. The fruit trees were bursting with fruit which the nuns would sell on Sundays after mass. They could afford the luxury of eating chicken once a week and pig's liver, a favourite with Mother Teresa. Now that there was less time for fun, Vera's presence became ever more necessary for the nuns. They anxiously awaited her arrival home from school. The system of little notes they passed on to one another had already become a habit in the chapel at four o'clock sharp.

'Has the girl arrived yet?'

'Who'll open the door?'

'Don't fret…'

Invariably the same questions and phrases were passed around as a series of notes until the final message.

'She's home, thank God.'

Vera not only was no bother to the community of Poor Clares in their austere lives, she irradiated something the nuns could not put a name to. It resembled on earth what they sought with their eyes turned towards the sky.

It was a sky that had begun to clear thanks to recent measures restructuring a new geographic and human landscape. A world in safe hands.

Unintentionally the cataclysm had seen the demise of most of those prone to violence, while the Third World War had then dealt with the remaining few who survived. A few corrupt regimes had disappeared almost immediately, toppled under their own weight or that of an irrefutable reality. National representatives in the World Government enforced regulations with little disagreement from each state. International conflicts were resolved by lawyers in complicated procedures at the International Criminal Court. The World Government imposed order through new laws, in some cases complied with through fear of financial or commercial penalties. Fear of extinction had become ingrained even in the minds of fanatics and nonconformists. The steady creation of millions of jobs bestowed purchasing power on everyone for the first time. The well-being of the majority had pushed aside that of the privileged minority. Citizens adapted easily to their good fortune.

Climbing the convent's bell tower was the only secret Vera kept from Benedita. As soon as she got in from school she would slam the door, which let the nuns in the chapel know she was back. Then she would run to the bell tower where nobody could see her climb to the top. She knew she had at least fifteen minutes before one of the nuns would cross herself and go and find her to ask how she had got on at school. Like a magnet, the height lead to that open space where the wind cleansed her. It was as essential to her as the long moonlit walks in the vegetable garden. In the bell tower, about to be taken over by a revelatory force, the beep of her watch alarm brought her back downstairs to the corridors of the convent that led to the dining room where she would have her tea. The rush left her breathless.

'You don't need to come running from school. Look at you, red as the tomatoes from the garden.'

Vera not only ran through the corridors but also

through the complex meanderings of digital technology. Mathematics held the same fascination for her as the energy she felt was released on a starry night. She studied science and at the same time experienced the phenomena she studied with a particular intuition that extended beyond the facts.

The time had come when not even Benedita was able to keep pace with her progress. The nuns had to make do with keeping up with her exam results. The content of the syllabus seemed as complicated to them as an astronomy or quantum physics textbook. Her adopted mothers were lost in shock at her sudden growth. Astonished as though they had had no childhood or had not advanced from that into puberty, which Vera was approaching with a new glow.

Vera no longer had time to help Benedita in the vegetable garden. From the huge windows she watched her and sister Leopoldina prepare the new seeds with their knees firmly on the ground. As she studied in front of the old computer, Vera did not know that she watched them with future nostalgia.

Curfews and restrictions on natural spaces had just been lifted when the technical school organised a picnic on the outskirts of Bari. Mesmerised by their electronic games, the children crowded together after lunch in the shade of the trees. Vera sat in front of the lake, watching the diminutive life on the shore, which was oblivious to the solar panels and wind turbines surrounding it. Without being withdrawn or distant, Vera was the quiet girl who excelled in class. She was unexpectedly serene. She absorbed her surroundings with a calmness that inhabited her effortlessly.

Like an oasis in the middle of the desert, the woods surrounded the lake at the end of three converging roads cutting through vast fields sown with metal spikes and huge terrestrial windows pointing to the sky. Even though it was hot, the children did not have permission to bathe in the lake. Precautions had been trebled in the natural environment. To the world's eyes nature had become the bearer of potential disasters. Its utilitarian use was strictly controlled without causing it any irreversible damage, like milk extracted to the last drop from an inseminated cow, distanced from her calf. The afternoon had passed almost unnoticed with the monotonous buzzing of the turbines, the occasional bird flying past.

'Children, children. Look, a bird. Quick! There! There it goes.'

The children hardly ever looked up but this was a special occasion.

'Look! A bird!'

They returned to their games unaware of the presence of nature all around them, one ignoring the other. The school curriculum stipulated that children devote the greater part of their free time to electronic games, using technology on which they would depend for leisure and, later, work. Now and then Vera was allowed to withdraw from the group. Being always ahead of the rest, it was a benefit she appreciated. The other children barely noticed her absence. They had already collected their little lunch boxes and dumped them in the recycling container. They had closed the portable food and drinks vending machine. The assistant stood in place to count the fifty-five children sitting in a row on the vinyl carpet under the trees at the edge of the lake. The head teacher also counted them. Fifty-four.

'I'm one short.'

'So am I.'

After counting twice more, the assistant took roll call to identify who was missing. Once identified, the head teacher sounded the alarm and called the school to inform them. The children knew the meaning of the high-pitched whistle, the implications of which they feared. Even if it was simply because of the disappearance of a hand control or the special signal prior to an important announcement on the general screen. The children would be startled by the break in routine. This time it was more serious. Galo had disappeared. The head teacher glanced accusingly at the assistant. He should be aware of the whereabouts of every child. They should not move from the vinyl carpet without being authorised to do so. It was ultimately his responsibility. Only Vera had been given that permission. Like the rest, Galo had collected his lunch box. He had not returned to the carpet like everyone else but had entered the woods to watch Vera without being seen. Galo wanted to be like her. He wanted to be different and to be allowed to sit facing the lake. He knew he could not justify that wish. Sitting on the edge of the forest, quietly observing Vera, Galo heard a rustling noise behind him. He turned to find a rabbit only a few meters away. Although he had never seen one in the flesh, he recognized it straightaway from cartoons and games. It looked and behaved very differently from the virtual alternatives he was familiar with. As soon as Galo stood up to take a closer look, the rabbit ran away and hid in a bush. He followed. It was Galo's first year at school but he knew the sound of the whistle well. Hearing it cut short the fascination which had pulled him deeper into the woods in chase of the rabbit. The whistle paralysed him. Not so the mischievous rabbit which did not react to the piercing sound in the same manner and ran away. 'Wait!' The rabbit didn't stop. Alone and confused by the echo among the treetops, Galo did not know which way to go. From a fantasy of tales lost in time, the woods had become a strange, inhospitable place.

The head teacher subjected not only the assistant but also the children to intense questioning. Vera had already rejoined the group as they were disposing of their empty boxes. None of the children had seen Galo. The sense of danger made a number of them cry, holding hands as they repeated 'Cataclysm, cataclysm!'. One could feel the disquiet in the air, which circulated thickly and made it difficult for the head teacher and her two assistants to breathe as they waited.

Absorbed in communications with the school and the police, the head teacher and her assistants did not notice Vera's temporary absence. When Vera found Galo he was sitting beneath a tree in silence, being brave, trying not to burst into tears. Vera took him by the hand and led him back to the group. The police had just arrived when they appeared hand in hand leaving everyone puzzled.

Nobody asked her how she had found him or how they had found their way out of the woods unaided. They did not even notify the convent. Unable to classify the event, the school committee could find no reason to scold or praise. Vera had disobeyed the rules so she should not be praised even though she had managed to rescue Galo from the woods. If she were to be praised, they would risk consenting to dangerous behaviour. In trying to understand this contradiction, the arguments back and forth in the lecture hall eluded the question which for a few moments left them in silence.

'How can this nine-year-old little girl have been able to find a seven-year-old boy in the middle of the woods without the aid of technology?'

The most sensitive exchanged brief glances. Others briefly opened their mouths and closed them again, staring at their hands. The more practical-minded agreed that this should not be the subject that concerned them. They should not lose focus. The question remained unanswered. Silence overwhelmed them then diffused into practical discussions about disciplinary measures.

The event was not even entered in school or police records. For Galo it had been the most important event of his life. At school Vera carried on as usual, although others now perceived her differently, without being able to specify how or why. Galo, meanwhile, reimmersed himself in his fantasy world. Vera had not only saved him but also become his friend. He, who was two years younger than she, he, who had become lost through carelessness. He, who had not been able to find his way out of the woods, he, who had wanted to be different. From the moment Vera had found Galo, they never separated again.

They would meet during school breaks. Although they did not seem out of place among the other children, absorbed in their games, Vera and Galo, hardly moving from where they sat, played outdated games – ones Vera had learned in the community and which she now taught Galo I-spy, noughts and crosses, cat's cradle. Vera surprised him with her ability to enjoy herself in the simplest ways, with no need to enter a manufactured universe not her own. They made up other games. Not only had they developed acumen as a result of bettering themselves through the skills of the other, but their insight had also allowed them to get to know their weaknesses and talents, their souls. Every day Galo went home to the orphanage and Vera to the convent.

In earlier years they waited for each other at the school gate. Later on as teenagers they would meet in front of the big screen that had been erected in the central square, where the World Government had begun broadcasting global news. Every morning, at the request of the local authorities, the population of every city in every nation would congregate before the thousands of screens newly installed in urban centres. Holding hands in the heart of Bari, Vera and Galo witnessed the changes announced in unison to the world's population.

Images of the Forty-Day War had long faded away. New screens were installed to show diverse informative clips. The World Government had to ensure that in every corner, however inhospitable, in every room, however private, in every mind, however absorbed, there was an awareness of the new rules and regulations and the success of the system:

'As promised, sustainable agriculture is our priority. We have prevented the disintegration of the food chain. Bee colonies are recovering. We are working towards the total elimination of the use of chemical pesticides. Every new home now complies with environmental regulations and existing buildings are being made greener, adapting them further for the use of human waste for gas production. Our next challenge will be to replace cables with nanotubes throughout a new supply network which will carry electricity with less impact to the environment. We made a promise and we are delivering. Armed conflict has been displaced by ingenuity and industry.'

At the technical school, once a week Vera and Galo had to attend screenings of World Government documentaries. The importance of young people becoming aware of the benefits of the new order was recognised. They had already learned about the latest events in contemporary history lessons. With a three-degree rise in temperatures in Africa, the Sudan, the Congo and Zimbabwe had become ghost countries. Students saw how US airplanes would arrive in the dust cloud of the dirt runways of airports as though through a mirage. From their airplane seats with expectant faces, those who had never before left their African villages showed off to the cameras their brand new personal electronic cards containing their full profile. Whole populations were being relocated to be trained in technology and factory production. Unwittingly, Vera and Galo saw how the vast halls of American universities were filled with African faces. They weren't to know that for the first time the highest salaries would go to those often-astonished faces. A few years on these same immigrants had become factory or IT employees. Many achieved what they used to yearn for as they stared at the TV screens of the poor neighbourhoods, shanty towns, slums, small villages; what the new order now offered them as an undeniable aspiration.

Over 200 million people had to be trained. The desire of taking part in the order and development of the world for the benefit of humanity was greater than ever. It was real. Men and women, all dressed the same in clean white T-shirts and jeans, arrived in American planes. In a succession of journeys from the land to the factory, from poverty to consumption, from local culture to world expansion. Slogans in even the remotest places on huge billboards proclaimed: 'We improve productivity and eliminate poverty. We offer you the marvels of technology and science for you and your family's health. Wholly environmentally friendly.' Everyone signed up to embrace a better life. A desire that now came together as a newly born association. The world also needed to drag them out of their misery. They needed each other. This time 'the others' would get their reward.

It had become as natural as it was expected that each day when they left school Galo would walk with Vera to the corner nearest the convent. Once nobody could see them, Galo would hold up the tablet level with their faces and kiss her on the lips. Together they were getting to know each other in a way that was new but familiar. He would run his hands through the ripples of her wavy brown hair while running his eyes along the soft lines of her cheeks easily tanned from hours spent outdoors. Vera would brush the silky hair on his arms with her open palm. The sense of touch was as primordial to her as was the sense of sight for Galo. Her eyes had an inescapable attraction for him. For Vera, it was Galo's smile that could move mountains.

Galo knew that the diligence with which Vera applied herself to her studies would have consequences that gave him concern. He was not yet fully aware that Vera would always be by his side. They talked of plans and dreams. They were so reluctant to part that Vera's new routine of arriving home late once again worried the nuns. They would be far more worried by her decision to continue her studies in Rome.

When she heard about Galo, Benedita struggled valiantly to hide her disappointment. More than any of the other nuns, she had secretly hoped that Vera would stay at the convent once she had completed her schooling. She had imagined what she knew to be impossible. Although she desired Vera's well-being, she had never had such contradictory feelings. These were new sins, unsuspected. Innocent sins that tormented her, as she hoped that her attachment to Vera would not stop her from feeling happy for the girl. While the priest consoled her, saying it was natural she should have these maternal feelings, he bit his tongue to avoid saying he had warned her.

She went straight to the point: 'Bless me, Father, for I have sinned. I think that what I feel is envy.' 'I'm not sure. Perhaps a little resentment too. Feelings that just come without me wanting them, Father… I've been poisoned…'

'Sister, Sister. You are too hard on yourself. I've already explained to you…'

'They are forbidden by God, Father.'

'It's all right, Sister. I will give you your penance. First it is important that you reflect…'

Each confession was like a therapy session. The patience of the nuns sitting on the pews at the back for Sunday confession was only matched by their deep understanding. They felt the same way, their feelings differing solely in intensity. The convent began to prepare for the unavoidable, although they never imagined it would come so soon.

It was not long before word reached Father Zillo of Vera's talents in the classroom. He had insisted on developing Vera's talent for computers while the convent was not in a position to provide her with a machine suitable for her studies. That was no obstacle for him. Knowing the weakness the nuns had for Vera, Father Zillo smuggled a laptop to them behind the Mother Superior's back. He had insisted that it should be a gift from them.

'You can pay me with your lemon tart,' he had said to Benedita. 'If you pay me, it's yours. What's yours belongs to the community, right?'

Benedita had warned him. The nuns did not want to put the Mother Superior in a situation where she would have to lie, even if it were a white lie. They had organised a lovely party. To please the nuns, she had at last bent down to whisper to the Mother Superior in her wheelchair.

'Reverend Mother, please don't be angry. Father Zillo gave us a laptop for Vera. He wants us to give it to her on behalf of the Order. You won't say anything, will you?'

There was no reply. The Mother Superior's seriousness worried Benedita as they sang a farewell song.

'I have something to say,' the Mother Superior tapped her spoon against her plate to call for silence after the applause and well-wishing. The nuns paused anxiously. As if hardly breathing. Mother Teresa passed the empty plate to Sister Gloria. The only sound was the squeaking of the worn tyres as she wheeled herself with difficulty towards Vera.

'Vera, we have taken you in like a daughter. That you owe, firstly, to Sister Benedita for her insistence.' The ensuing laughter relaxed Benedita momentarily. 'And then to yourself, your good heart. I know we'll be seeing much less of you. You've not long to go now. The world outside this house is a tough one. Don't lose your soul, child.'

The Mother Superior gestured to Benedita, who immediately approached with the parcel. When she put it on her lap, Mother Teresa squeezed her hand with a fondness that only she knew how to interpret. When she addressed Vera lifting the parcel like an offering, the nuns appeared to shrink around her.

'Vera, we'd like to give you this present so that you don't forget us.'

It was inevitable that Vera would join the Vatican's IT Academy. On graduating with honours from technical school, the nuns' joy at Vera's top grades did not make her departure any easier. Nor did they help relieve their loneliness in the convent. Although the nuns' fear that she was too young to go out into the world was understandable,

Vera was confident they would let her go. This time Galo's presence would have a positive, reassuring effect on the community. Galo could keep a close eye on her. He had received the acceptance letter to be transferred to the Shelterbase refuge in Rome. Galo had promised to follow her to the end of the world.

Like a diminutive unnoticed island in the new global ocean, the Poor Clare community understood more than ever the need to safeguard the convent. In the past the difficulties faced by the Church had barely been suspected by the community. Now rumours about the closure of several convents gained greater significance when new information began to appear on the urban screens. There was only one person they could turn to. It was no coincidence that Father Zillo had been withdrawn from their lives for months. The Vatican depended on him more and more for its survival, having had to compensate thousands of victims of abuse with hundreds of millions of dollars. Despite herself, the Mother Superior decided to bother Father Zillo, having read a leaflet that dropped through the letter box. His words to her offered some comfort.

'The World Government is imposing strict regulations to all churches and religions. But that doesn't mean that they can close the convent, Mother.' Father Zillo tried to be reassuring, but he himself had strong concerns.

'The exclusive promotion of one religion has been banned.' Mother Teresa quoted from the leaflet.

'I understand your apprehension, but the government equally guarantees that any hostility or discrimination against any religion is illegal and will be heavily penalised. The main reason is to safeguard against the proven danger posed by out-of-control fanaticism. They have no intention to affect religious traditions. There will be a summit on World Religions soon and all representatives will have a say.'

Father Zillo was right, but he could not have predicted

that the World Government would go further than this. During the summit, it would go on to create a Single World Church which was announced as the supreme triumph of neodemocracy. With the World Church as an instrument of social cohesion and harmony, integration would be complete. Its only purpose was to provide balance for those who lacked it, an instrument for those who had not managed to overcome the fear of death. Religion, an item of personal need rather than moral scales for the masses, had finally been separated from the State. Morality was now in the hands of justice under the protective wing of corporate governments. The dissociation of church and state meant an end to the beatings and executions in the name of God. Submission to husbands, parents, clergymen in the name of God. The impositions on the female body in the name of God. That ancient God had also disappeared with the initial perception that the Apocalypse had already happened. The surviving population had been given a second opportunity. In time religion would be substituted by products filling the spiritual world.

For Vera religion had not been a personal need. It was not a social or cultural choice. It was neither good nor bad. Religion was her family. What nourished her was what she had discovered in the convent's vegetable garden. The blue in the distance exerted a perfect, silent pull at her very core, imbuing her with meaning. The moon had overseen her birth and ever since had watched her grow in its source, just as she naturally withdrew from everything that seemed superfluous to her at the convent. The world around her also seemed much more distant than the sea on the horizon.

In Rome, Vera devoted herself fully to her studies and to Galo so that life in the great city would not absorb her. There the rules were stricter, the limits more defined. On occasion they plunged her into a desire to be alone that was difficult for her to unravel.

'So, are we not seeing each other today, then? Shall we talk later before you go to bed?,' Galo knew he could only ask her once. After that he had to leave her alone.

'Not today, Galo.'

'We can study together whenever you like. Just let me know.'

If he did not hear from her for a few days, Galo would try again.

'Do you miss the convent? I too sometimes think of returning to Bari but I like my new course. Here everything is much more advanced.' If he chatted to her, he knew Vera would finally come out of her state of separation. 'I'll go with you to Bari at the weekend, if you like.'

'No. Let's go to the country. I heard they're shutting off access to some places again.'

'Perfect. I have something for you. Saturday at ten o'clock.'

Galo had been saving for months from his scholarship money. He knew that once Vera sat for her last exam she would return to the convent. He asked her to meet him by the side gate of his lodging house at Shelterbase. He stood leaning against the railings with his bike when she approached him. They greeted each other with a kiss and had only walked a few metres along the railing when Vera stopped.

'Isn't it beautiful?' Vera admired a striking blue brand new bicycle which was secured to the railing, while Galo watched her with a big smile on his face. His plan had worked perfectly well.

'It's not only beautiful. It's yours.' Galo held out a small key for the lock.

She stood in silence with open eyes, admiring both the bicycle and Galo's smile.

'Go on! I have planned a long ride for today.

Vera threw her arms around Galo's neck and squeezed so hard that he yelped in a mixture of excitement and discomfort.

He was so pleased with himself. They would not need to rent a bicycle for her anymore. They could go anywhere together, if Vera stayed by his side.

When Vera returned to the convent a month later, Galo did not know what to think. He was aware that the nuns would rather have Vera stay with them. He had not imagined that Father Zillo would be the one to bring Vera back to Rome and back to him, finally putting his mind at rest. Now head of Vatican Inc., Father Zillo arrived at the convent to ask for the Mother Superior's approval.

'She'll be in the very best hands. You wouldn't want to deny her such an opportunity. Our work demands the highest level of security in selecting staff. Trust in our programmers is paramount, Reverend Mother. Not only the quality of their work and their creative talent, but also their absolute discretion. We don't often have a vacancy. This young lady is the best candidate of all the IT students.'

Vera's eyes were smiling when at last Father Zillo came out of the office with Benedita and the Mother Superior.

'My dear, welcome to the heart of the Vatican,' he stretched his arms out to her. 'It is yours now. You have one of the most coveted posts in IT. Although I don't doubt that you're well aware that coveting is no virtue,' he smiled at the nuns as he squeezed both her hands between his.

Benedita could feel pleased with herself. She had achieved what had been her aim from the first day she saw Vera at the old lady's house. Her task had not been on a whim, nor was it an imposition or a charitable duty. Benedita had seen what the old lady's watery eyes could not. On Alina's altar, pinned to the rubber helmet was a note written in handwriting that was shaky from weakness and lack of habit: 'Save Vera'. Her mother had also placed a box with her belongings in it next to the cot. As though getting ready to leave, she had lain down fully dressed with her shoes and coat on. That was how Benedita had found her. She had shown the old lady the box and had placed the things from the altar inside the handkerchief which Vera's mother held tightly in her hand. The old lady had been right to believe that there must be a reason for such an absurd death.

Alina had also managed to carry out her mission. She had managed to leave and give birth in spite of being raped by her step-father, to the indifference of her mother. She had managed to transform the repulsive into the admirable and the ignoble into the exceptional. Above all, she had transformed danger into safety. The notebook found among her few clothes explained more than Vera would have liked to know. Pages written in childish handwriting revealed an adult life which had no meaning other than the horror within the farm walls, her life clearly divided in two: before and after Vera's birth.

Vera, who had been conceived against all desire, had been born against all odds, had survived against all probability and had grown contrary to every rule. At eighteen years old, the same age at which her mother had died, Vera the IT expert joined the staff at the Vatican's software company.

PART III

population with updates on international pacts and the rapid political modernisation of countries with a troubled past. Alliances were not reinforced from the heavens under divine promises, but in the nearest regions of the cosmos. In the silence of space, remote controlled orbital spacecraft guarded the earth from the stars. One complete orbit every sixty minutes. Watchdog satellites loaded with radars did not leave a single area open to the unexpected. The World Government's optical recognition was absolute. Security had become the new religion.

When Vera left the convent for good she had no idea that her birth had marked a division between the world into which she had been born and that to which she was being delivered by the nuns eighteen years later. Now that the horror was over there was just the reality of the present in charge of erasing all awareness. Human and financial resources were at the service of the ephemeral end product. The population followed trends, like organised ants for a common good: survival. With technological science as the third element of the trinitarian faith, 'Security, Entertainment and Technology' became the Holy Trinity that conditioned society against the fear of further threats. The world was less subtle. In no time tribes, cultures, traditions, idiosyncrasies had been flattened into a uniform human layer.

Vera did not know the reason for the widespread lack of any verve for life. Everyone wanted to forget, she concluded. She was born on the day of the cataclysm. She had been as close or closer to death than anyone else. Vera struggled to feel part of the buzz around her. She was not attracted to the mechanical innovation of entertainment. The solace of free time, they called it. It had arrived in the golden age of individual growth and reward, this dedication to paid work and well-deserved rest: the longest free time in the history of paid employment in the digital age. A phrase she had read years ago in one of the convent books had never left her: 'The search for the sublime'. It made her reflect more than ever. Had the sublime, then, been found by mankind within a life of material growth? Vera did not feel nourished by devices or their associated consumables which raised expectations to unreachable heights in the insatiable search for satisfaction. Her aspirations were not that high. More than anything else, Vera realised that the world was alien to her. Although her knowledge of it was so profound that it seemed completely natural, she found herself wholly outside this world which so absorbed everyone. Within and outside herself at the same time, Vera dreamed of worlds that could be explained solely by intuition. The world containing her in matter and spirit related to her flesh, her breathing and her senses. To feel complete, Vera devoted herself to the little natural environment that still remained. Nothing that she saw outside that environment which enveloped her was sacred so she rarely mentioned it for fear that it would also be taken over and sold like everything else. That which fulfilled Vera represented to the rest a potential for industrial exploitation or highly controlled tourism. Limited by the carbon emission quota, travelling had a motive so distant from her own that Vera felt as isolated from her environment as she was immersed in it. Alienated though sensible. Confused though lucid. She avoided being affected by anything other than that which shaped her essence. It was only Galo who knew this. He was the one Vera had found without effort. Galo shared the intimacy with a woman sensitive to events of which he had no intuition, although he admired them. He accompanied her as she welcomed under her feet the crackling of the leaves, the stones charged with cosmic history, with reality. If the world shied away from reality, she would relate to it in silence, privately.

Since they had moved into the apartment, Vera would stick around the walls of their room the pictures from places they discovered together. Most of them had been fenced off. Access was restricted and controlled following postcataclysmic new rules.

Whilst Galo was editing a photo, Vera was searching satellite images. It was a usual weekend.

'It doesn't seem to be fenced. It's fourteen kilometres away. Are you ready?' Vera put the SatNav inside her small rucksack.

Galo printed the picture and gave it to Vera. She looked at it closely. The wind turbines were screened behind the trees, veiled thanks to the dexterity of the photographer and his skilful editing.

'Looks great.' She kissed him holding him around the waist.

'Are we staying in?' Galo joked.

They hid their bikes in a bush close to the path. They walked through the forest for a while until they reached the meadow shown by the satellite image. It did not reveal the most up to date picture of the area. Even knowing that, Vera did not expect to see the industrial complex for the deposit and recycling of metals. Nor did she expect to find that the hills had been sliced through to become a gaping quarry.

'This is as far as we can walk. Let's go.' Galo laid his hand on Vera's shoulder. Her disappointment was not the only thing that unsettled him. Almost certainly there would be a surrounding electronic fence. 'We'll find other places. Let's eat something and leave.'

They sat down in the darkness of the forest, as if it would be the only natural place outside the city where they could be alone that morning, feeling that the world was theirs. They sat close together against a tree and quietly ate some food before heading back.

Once home, Galo produced a small yellow flower with a long thin stem, which he threaded through her tied up hair. These were the times when Galo took great care to make her smile. Vera hugged him and rested her head on his shoulder, letting herself appreciate the sweet scent on his neck.

'I said we should stay at home.' Although this time he was not joking, Vera laughed while Galo lifted her up to carry her to the bedroom.

There, as in the convent tower, the world did not exist. Only the senses that stirred the emotions they shared and made them one. His restorative embrace would always bring her back to the good fortune of their lives together.

Galo had gone from admirer to friend to boyfriend, eventually being everything to her.

Vera had avoided taking him to the convent not so much because visitors were not allowed inside the cloister, but because she understood the nuns' reservations and sensed Benedita's jealousy of Galo. She had no wish to be ungrateful. It would seem to her that indeed she would be if she brought inside the walls which safeguarded self-denial and devotion the young man who had taken her away. She never stopped telling them stories about him, through which the nuns would still come to know him well. They were relieved to know without seeing, to accept without having to tolerate. As though her Prince Charming were merely that, a fantasy which would one day return to a storybook once the last page was turned.

They saw her on the occasional weekend, then over time weekends at the convent became a few daytime hours. Vera's bed seemed so large that Benedita piled things on it in order not to see it. After a few months the Mother Superior decided to intervene in order to help her overcome Vera's absence. One afternoon, when Benedita had come back from the vegetable garden, she took her by the hand and led her to the first floor. On opening the door of her old room, a jug with daisies from the garden and a card were there waiting for her. 'Sister, we miss you. These corridors are lifeless without your presence.' Once Benedita returned to her old room everything seemed more natural and spontaneous. Memories became less painful with Benedita once again sharing with them their same routine. The nuns even seemed to forget that Vera had once been in their care. As if she were an enchanted princess, they became used to the idea that, by the same magic with which she had appeared in their lives, she had now vanished. They were left with a sweet aftertaste and a smile brought on by the rare occasions when news of her reached them.

PART IV

Vera and Galo did not celebrate anniversaries or remember dates. They lived one day at a time with the same light-heartedness that fuelled their dreams of other places and other people. It had been almost eleven years since they had moved in together. It had not been difficult to make the transition from childhood to adolescence and thence to maturity. Like so many others, they had finished their technology studies, at which they excelled, Vera as an expert programmer specialising in digital games, Galo as a lecturer in support technology. She was the software and he was the hardware they joked between themselves. There was a greater difference that nobody knew and that was their secret. Whilst the rest of humanity switched on their consoles after work, they switched off and got ready for the next day. Every morning the world was transformed into whatever they wanted of it. They would set out at dawn in search of places uninhabited by technology; natural oases with no turbines, panels, sensors, geothermal systems, storage plants, micro-reactors or processors. For them the most beautiful place was a sanctuary where no other sound could be heard that was not natural to the surroundings. Vera and Galo. Their names were not on the long waiting lists to visit nature reserves established as huge gardens. There what was natural did not form part of nature. Wildlife had also been organised to maximise its procreation and equilibrium among species. Visits were guided and time and space limited. From watering systems, module-based food chain or wildlife and floral zones, nothing was left to nature. Reserves were an operating theatre for the care of animal and vegetable species. From the ground ready for sowing to the so-called 'green fields', destined for green technology, they were perfect, unblemished zones. Vera and Galo wandered free, in the few areas they found which were not involved in the extraordinary organisation of life. Forbidden places where nobody wanted to venture in or dared do so. It was a shared adventure to feel part of the beginning of time.

Vera and Galo lived in a near perfect world planned for success. It was said that mankind had never before been as free. With whole populations travelling towards new possibilities, there was extraordinary mobility. The news no longer centred on biofuels or competition between foodstuffs and hydrocarbons. Reporting nowadays was about changes in the market for digital games. Everybody signed up to work for the saviour industry. Marketing science was taught in all schools. The most solid foundation. The only one. Games were there to fill time. Distraction was an essential tool in the organization of life, its value proven across the centuries. For the Roman poor, the circus had offered consolation against hunger and disease, a ploy for a more bearable life. In front of the computer the feeling of well-being depended on games and their processed reality to permeate the senses. The entertainment-based economy had been the new spring for the final jump. The few who saw it as a jump into the void lived on the edges. The new, inclusive and fair environmental, social and labour laws had invalidated activists' arguments against the new order. Paralysing conformism had turned into indifference. The critical analysis of the past had melted in the political cauldron of the market. Hard facts were the only ones worthy of comment. Efficiency and productivity were the end point in the search for truth.

As the Vatican's financial investor, Zillo had rarely worn a cassock. If it had not been conducive to business before the cataclysm, afterwards it was actually counterproductive. Seeing him sitting with a group in the Budbar nobody would suspect that the man, who looked like a City high-flyer, was as devout as any other priest devoted to less mundane tasks. Zillo knew very well the world of business and its stereotypes. That was why he could often be seen with a glass in hand, although he never drank a drop of alcohol. Every year he would gather a few business friends together in his favourite bar to invite them to the Vatican for his birthday. It was essential that he lived in the city of investment. He travelled the world in a private jet at his disposal. Twice a week he flew to the Vatican to propose or report on investments, their potential or their results. Not even the huge losses suffered in the financial debacle managed to weaken his position. The trust the Vatican had in him was unshakable. When donations dried up and the choice was between keeping the hundreds of thousands of churches, parishes and convents all over the world burning the Vatican's riches, or closing them down, it was Zillo who had the vision to give the Vatican the cybernetic push it needed. Vatican Software Inc. was the first cyber company linked to a religious body. Once the World Church had granted authorisation and created the regulations to restrict it, all the others followed suit. It was a case of adapt or die. His task was not only to create a new world of games for those with eyes on the Vatican, but also to recruit new members. Although Zillo thought of them as parishioners, they were more like followers or voters. The difficulty was not in finding an ally, he had one. Zillo's greatest challenge was showing dissent against the decision of the Vatican council to hire the most renowned games creator in the industry. They did not realise the foolishness of their plans to invite someone from outside the community. Although opposed to his ideas, the council listened to him attentively.

'We cannot risk knowledge of the code being in the hands of an outsider, however brilliant they are. Without total commitment there is no loyalty.'

'Without quality, there is no preponderance,' was the favoured cardinal's reply.

'I can guarantee both' Zillo was putting his career on the line.

It was above all a profound faith that inspired him, with no fear or compromise. The Pope's vote of confidence was the first step in putting total control in his hands. Any doubts were dispelled by immediate sales results and customer devotion to the many games created. Zillo had forged a solid alliance headed by Carda, his protégé. The king of games was not long in arriving. *Vatican World I* was more than a resounding success. The Vatican's coffers filled once more and the Church once again became a key player.

'I'm too old for travelling and partying,' Zillo had said to Carda when he placed him at the head of the development division. 'No other investment could reverse our falling income. The cataclysm was our *coup de grâce*. In fact, the first World Government was. If it had been up to them, no temple would have been left standing. It will be my best investment. We're not allowed to spread the creed, but nobody can prevent us from advertising our products. This is our chance to change course to something more in agreement with the laws of the universe.'

Carda was still awaiting his opportunity, after Zillo had broadened the Vatican's business interests by entering the games market. He had been one of the first graduates of the Vatican's IT Academy. He had a set expression which Zillo knew well. He was also aware of Carda's exceptional talent. He had been leader of the development team. The designer's ideas were kept secret until the last minute. The code was spread among a handful of programmers so as to keep from them the overall design of the final product until its launch. Industrial espionage among software companies was commonplace but very hard to prove due to the hundreds of thousands of products trying to imitate each other and win new fans. The race to innovate was unstoppable, its function not so much a notion of progress as control of the market. Like a snowball, innovation would gather together whatever it needed in order to grow. It would flatten everything in its path.

When Zillo called Carda many years later, he was not expecting it. Things had changed. After the remarkable success of *Vatican World I* and the development of many other peripheral games, to Zillo's disappointment, Carda had requested a transfer to the research department.

He could hardly remember the last time he had been asked to meet Zillo in the Budbar. Carda knew very well how to hide his nervousness. There he was again, listening to Zillo's 'homilies' as he called them.

'To be in the lead is everything. The World Church doesn't exist. We are still set against each other, but the World Government won't admit it. They tell me they're trivial disputes, that what matters is market leadership, that the Vatican has other important products… blah, blah, blah. They say that but they don't realise it's artificial, like everything they've created. Religion is the most important spiritual guide and it's been shoved into a corner. They're worse than gamblers. They play for high stakes. Until they lose everything. A chain of ups and downs. They think the world is a casino where you can gamble your future. With no meaning, no knowledge, no philosophy. There is no poetry. It's all politics and business. They only see regulations for production and well-being. People merely as producers and consumers.'

'I see you've dusted down your cassock.'

'A sign of the times. Who knows whether good or bad. Profound transformations should be instigated by profound processes.'

'I suppose you have something important to tell me.'

Carda's harshness gave Zillo the answer he had been hoping for. He had not changed. He could trust him.

'I have a meeting with the Council. I'm going to nominate you for our most ambitious project yet. It's not simply another version of the game. It's not just about gaining a prominent position once more, but beating every sales record. Not only among our products, but any products. I want to put you in charge. Are you ready for that?'

He had been mistaken. His chance had come at last.

'Of course I am.'

While sitting in the waiting room Vera could already see Father Zillo on the screen next to the electoral candidate. Galo had pointed him out to her:

'Yes, that's him. His hair's gone white.'

'I told you so.'

'He'll be in Development.'

'He's back. They probably want to launch something bigger.'

When the presidential candidate disengaged himself from Father Zillo's arm, waving his hands to thousands of followers, their voices could still be heard as they unclipped the microphones from their lapels. The technician was turning off the lights on the blue screen which had been overlaid with the image of thousands of voters with banners displaying the names of the companies and their candidates. The political message was broadcast instantaneously and live from the office. Reproducing well-attended rallies with only two or three politicians appearing live was routine to Zillo. The appropriate background varied according to the time of year. When the door opened and Zillo saw Vera come in, the technician was rolling up the blue screen.

'My dear. It's lovely to see you.' With a gesture the priest turned impatiently. 'Roch, leave that for now.'

The technician left the office and closed the door.

'I won't hold it against you if you don't remember me. Who's going to remember a bad-tempered old man! Just seeing you has brightened up my day. Your work has been impeccable. It's time to give you a responsibility worthy of your maturity and talent. You'll be working with an excellent team. I'm in charge so we'll be near each other.'

He again squeezed her hands. He looked at her with his eyes opened wide and eyebrows raised, adding a redundant emphasis to his words.

'It's the new version of *Vatican World*,' he told her.

Vera was well aware of the importance of the company's top game. Zillo went to his desk and pressed one of the buttons on the panel to his left.

'Is he here yet?'

'He's just arrived, Father. I'll show him in.' The voice sounded as if it came from the roof, filling every space of the ample room.

'Come.' Zillo took Vera's arm and led her to the back of the office.

On the other side of the panelled window there were rows and rows of terminals with hundreds of IT operators. Father Zillo had a panoramic view of the vast processing room from above, whilst the operators could only see the news and instructions projected onto their side of the giant multi-faceted window panes.

'Impressive, isn't it? This is where *Vatican World* has been developing. At first the programmers were also on this floor. Now they work behind closed doors. That's where you'll be. What you see below is only the service staff. The corridor separates the support staff from the online update staff.'

The sound of footsteps behind her did not distract Vera from the image of that sea of heads which, were it not for the screens in front of them, would not glow at all.

'Another great talent. Felix, do come in.'

Carda and Zillo met in the middle of the room. Vera had still not torn her eyes away from the expressionless faces below. When the priest embraced Carda effusively, he received little response.

'Welcome. It's been approved. It will be a pleasure to work with you again.'

Carda's silence did not bother Zillo.

'Vera, my dear. Come. Mr Carda will be your new boss. He has been the soul of *Vatican World*, its designer. I prefer to say its father. But many would accuse me of being mawkish. Now he's the new Director of Development for the latest version. For the sake of security, part of the code will be written in our office in New York to be compiled at Headquarters. The rest is in your hands, Felix. Just as before. Vera has worked on our less prestigious products in the annex offices. It's time she was given more responsibility. The importance of confidentiality at this particular time goes without saying. The competition is relentless. The last version of *Islamic World* sold more than our game thanks to its "surprise option".'

Vera could not guess whether Carda's set expression had more to do with efficiency and responsibility than annoyance.

'Each level has a "surprise option",' he explained, 'which can be activated a maximum of five times a day and creates a special expectation. A dependence on the game as never before. The surprises are different each time, truly unique.'

'Well,' Father Zillo interrupted him with a smile. 'Our *Cf* version of *Vatican World* is designed to win over the market. And that's what will happen.' He tried to soften Carda's furrowed brow by slapping him on the back.

'Otherwise we'll lose the party's approval,' added Carda, his face impassive.

It was not that the new world order had achieved a newborn awareness. As though a universal epiphany lit up the path to understanding the world in a new way. The digital age was the new industrial age. Wars were a thing of the past but images of violence and death were still present. Aggression, far from being an option in the real world, would take shape in the virtual world. Like a reminder of the danger, they said. Ideas had not changed. Death on a global scale had not managed to sweep away the notions that had given rise to it. Events made into entertainment dissociated violence from the events themselves. Battles, deaths, mutilations, destruction. The digital universe inside a perfect box. 'It must exert a more powerful attraction than perfume,' was Zillo's instruction to the designer. The product was the distillation of a perfect perfume in an attractive box. Games above life. People had nothing to say, their lips kept sealed by the creation of other lives, independent, free, exciting, rebellious and even criminal. The lives of the avatars.

The population was a huge, insatiable customer sitting at the edge of an increasingly unsuspected universe. In peace the world was the promised land where poverty had been replaced by the consumption of devices for distraction and entertainment; the long-awaited new version. Each product was endlessly transformed. Technology had saved humanity. Everything could be bought, sold or rented: products, companies, technology, organs, services, blood, labour, sperm, sex, wombs, leisure, genes, politicians, alliances. Like an oiled machine, neo-democracy worked automatically with the control of the World Bank and brand-name companies. Politicians were their faces. At the least sign of conflict, the financier/producer State implemented mechanisms of world security and legislation. The press, politicians, the clergy, rulers, all their servants. There were no conflicts of interest because they shared a common interest: the avoidance of conflict.

The new world was started with a clean slate. Vera and Galo had already learned things differently. History seemed to be covered with a filtering veil. Books from the past talked about things nobody read about. Books had been summarised on digital plates. Texts from the past were no longer comprehensible. Paper books were kept as valuable items like platonic objects of which only their shadows are seen. The digital shadows of distinguished volumes condensed their stories to turn them into outlines.

Several of the long narratives which expounded on past life were reduced to some ten pages of script and made into games. *Crime and Punishment, The Odyssey, Alice in Wonderland, Macbeth, The Divine Comedy, Gulliver's Travels, Paradise Lost, Hamlet, The Iliad, The Thousand and One Nights, Don Quixote de la Mancha, Great Expectations* and hundreds of others provided the action for absorbing games. Not in terms of their content but in their visual capacity for a plot full of exploits. The desire to know and understand had been displaced by the desire to play. Knowledge beyond technology or science had gone from being dangerous to being useless.

PART V

Seated in front of their screens, hundreds of people stared at the projection on the window panels of Zillo's office. It had been a while since they had been addressed by the Pope. From investor for the Church, Zillo had risen to General Manager of Vatican Software Inc. He was the voice which the Vatican needed in order to survive. With Carda's assistance he had helped achieve a goal of prominence for the Church that he long-desired for it. This status was fragile. Like everything else it was the result of a sustained battle against the competition. Above all, it was a product of the efforts and the vision of a few minds of greater insight. In the office Roch received the signal from Zillo, who raised his arms as though addressing the Pope on his balcony. The camera began to broadcast. The images merged in real time.

'When I reported to the Pope that we had reached a point at which even our own parishioners were buying *Islamic World*, he granted me authorisation. And here it is.' Zillo raised the brand new box of the new version of *Vatican World*.

He could not help but smile at the ovation as he stretched his hands out in front of him, gesturing for silence.

'With the help of my dearest and most talented programmers here beside me, we will reach every home that has been waiting for this message. We have lost valuable ground. We will now win it back. Knowledge is generated by millions of people working to that end. You are the reason for and source of that knowledge. It is within everyone's reach. To you I say "thank you". For your involvement in the order and development of the world. For the happiness of the entire population. Here it is. The key to truth,' Zillo raised the access key to *Vatican World Cf*.

The clamour of the crowd in the square was deafening. The Pope gave a final wave, while the first images of the game merged into that of Zillo standing alongside his hundreds of waving operators all wearing almost perfect smiles. Thousands of people in the square waved their arms in return. Both the display at central office and the huge screen next to the Papal balcony were split to broadcast both images. Side by side, united in common joy in an almost fraternal embrace. Neither the users in the square at the feet of the Pope nor the IT workers at Zillo's feet could hide their excitement. They provided the means to the well-being of society. As the game gradually took over the whole screen, little by little the crowd began to form an admirable queue. Thousands of well-behaved fans approached the stands under the balcony of St Peter's Basilica eager to buy the first boxes of *Vatican World Cf.*

The sound of a box landing on the table woke Galo. He had fallen asleep on the sofa with the screen on. In a reflex action, his arm lifted the hand control to turn it off.

'How was the launch?'

'Zillo wouldn't let me leave. The poor man wanted to make sure I got the same recognition as Carda.'

'As if you cared.'

'Carda obviously did.'

'Same face?'

'Even in the middle of a reception he is unable to hide his displeasure. The more Zillo praises me…'

Galo got off the sofa to embrace her with one arm while with the other he lifted the shiny box which contained the access key, the control glove, the special sensor and the projection card.

'My little genius.'

'Not only does it have the "surprise option", each projection card is loaded with secondary characters, secret weapons, additional locations and much more,' Vera imitated Carda's deep voice.

'Now he'll leave you in peace.'

'I hope they assign him to another project. Zillo wants me to be Head of Support.' Vera took the box from his hand. She held it up in the air while Galo opened the trunk that was against the wall. She dropped it onto dozens of other boxes with access keys, cards, controls and consoles, which would remain buried under a red cloth.

When Vera had got home that night nothing had changed except for Galo's hours at the technical college. They had hardly ever argued. They did not really know how to. Vera's prolonged silence was unlike any other he´d come across before. When she did not look him in the eye, he knew she was annoyed.

'I knew you'd object.'

'Doesn't it bother you?'

'It's six months. They compensate me for the change more than generously. This could be our chance to go away and live the life we want.'

The words were piling up inside Vera's head. Words were not her realm and she found it difficult to put them in order. She preferred to be concise, keeping thoughts to herself only to express what she had concluded. Galo had learned to be patient. Vera went over to the window, where she usually felt better.

'The opportunity has always been there.'

'So has my insecurity. Go ahead, say it, I don't mind.'

Galo went up to her hesitantly and took her hand to bring her towards him and hold her close.

'If we continue exploring, we can make it bearable.'

'Time will fly, I'm sure.'

Resentment was not a feeling Vera was familiar with. For the first few weeks of his new schedule Galo would find a note in his pocket each morning. 'Last night I was watching you as you slept. It seemed like time had stopped.' The next day, 'Think of a cloud and a treetop,' and the one after that, 'that's what we are.'

She would accompany Galo to the station before cycling

to one of the usual natural refuges or in search of a new one. Vera roamed around the periphery of production on unoccupied land, a sort of limbo, where all her doubts were dispelled. Every day she left for work before one in the afternoon and Galo arrived home before two. Official shifts from eight until one and from two until seven -the new global law. People had to live close to their workplace. No more than five stops away. Schedules ruled everyone and everything. Leisure time rewarded the work of satisfied employees fairly. They had never been given so much. Screen technology offered endless possibilities for taking care of time. On the one hand, work-induced stress and related conditions of the past had been swept away thanks to increased personal time. On the other, free time flew by with all the entertainment on offer. Hundreds of avenues opened up with games fulfilling lives, desires, aspirations. To eradicate all possibility of boredom and its consequences, entertainment prevented the hours from becoming disconcertingly permeable to the unknown.

Galo made an effort to visit the spaces they shared. They had promised each other not to abandon the routine which gave meaning to their lives. Each in the absence of the other. Together in their purpose until the day's end. But Galo's loneliness was barely relieved by the pleasure of contact with nature. For him, the only thing that made sense was Vera's presence. Without her, places brought back feelings of discomfort and the distress he had felt on the day he had got lost in the woods. Without telling her, Galo would return earlier each afternoon and wait in the flat. It was a long wait. He knew Vera would want to hear the story of some discovery or other, however small. She would ask for descriptions which Galo could not give her of spots he had never visited. When *she* discovered anything new, she would give him the coordinates and explain how to get there.

'You know how it is. The thought of getting lost makes me nervous,' he tested her reaction.

'Are you going to remain cooped up all that time?'

The fear of disappointing Vera made him lie.

'If you don't mind, I'll only go to our refuge. I prefer to wait until we go exploring together again. We both know I'm not much good at finding my way back. You wouldn't want to lose me,' he joked.

Vera, on the other hand, lived for the end of the day when she could tell him where she had been and what she had seen. She had made a map of the region and marked every detail on it. To show him.

'The woods south of Marcigliana.'

'Yes.'

'Didn't you go there yesterday?'

'Yes…'

'Didn't you see the cameras? They've installed cameras. Did you get beyond the perimeter?'

'I didn't actually go in. I thought you wouldn't be going back for now.' The excuses would do. Just.

'There are no places left. There are more and more cameras,' Vera distracted herself from Galo's fudged attempts at avoiding the issue. She shuddered at the knowledge that security continued to restrict green spaces.

'I'm worried that you'll be found out and told off.'

'For sitting and looking at what nobody's interested in.'

'Promise me you won't do anything too risky.'

'What do you think might happen? That they implant an ID sensor. I don't think they can override the company.'

'The company or the rest of them. It's all the same.'

Galo choked on the question he could not ask her: was it worth the risk?

Although the hours of rest were long, for Vera the time was too short. She was absorbed in a world which took her further and further away from the hall saturated with screens. She could sense a huge gap, invisible like an immense ghostly structure. Something that widened around her until she felt the void which could suck her in and make her disappear. As if the air were not made up only of oxygen and other gases but of dark spaces with no energy, no force. With nothing to breathe.

A few days after the launch, Carda called her out of the development room. He held a magnetic card up in the air at the height of Vera's face. No response.

'Your own office. Congratulations.'

In normal circumstances Carda would not have expected Vera to share with him her joy or satisfaction. He was not surprised that this time it was no different. He gave her a few seconds in case she had anything to say. Vera lifted her open hand and Carda dropped the card into it.

'You will also have greater access to the system. And naturally, greater responsibility over the staff. I'm no longer your boss. Zillo asked me to explain procedures and the system to you. I know it very well. Now you will get to know it.'

'If it's not absolutely necess...'

'It is. You'll have limited access. It's all divided into modules. Nobody has complete access.'

He went with her to the office. At the end of the corridor he stopped in front of two adjacent doors.

'The other one is my office. I'm in charge of the *Cf* updates. Until the next project.'

Vera could not tell whether Carda had noticed her disappointment. He opened the door with his master pass card as if it belonged to him. Vera entered and waited next to the door for Carda to leave. Carda did not misinterpret Vera's immobility. Saying nothing, he coolly went up to the brand new screen on the desk. He lifted his thumb to activate the sensor disregarding the feeling that he was not welcome. The jumble of Vera's thoughts was crushing her between the temples. So much so that she might not be able to help them burst out, even if for the first time. Aware of this, Carda would push Vera to her limits and without giving her time to explore them, he would pull her right back. She had never been forced beyond those limits. It was only a matter of seconds before he would give Vera something that she could hold on to so as to dissipate her rage, which restored her to normality. It was a game Carda repeated as if to put her to the test.

'Once the threshold has opened you'll be able to record your V-pass.'

The screen lit up right away. Carda went up close to look into the tiny camera. He leant on the back of the empty chair. Vera followed his movements with a heightened awareness. She could not tell whether Carda entered the changes while standing as a sign of respect or tolerance. Still she did not offer him to sit.

'You can now register your V-pass.'

Despite gravity weighing her down like lead, Vera, ethereal, reluctantly dragged her feet to the table. She stared at the screen and lifted her thumb in front of it. Immediately a voice welcomed her.

'My V-pass has been erased as you registered yours. Now nobody but you will be able to authorise access to your terminal. This time there are two passwords. Martino's orders. Security enhancement. You can register them at the end.'

Carda took Vera's silence to be like his own.

'Sit down, please.'

She sat in front of the keyboard while Carda remained standing behind her, reflected in the screen like a faint shadow.

'You'll have access to avatar interconnection so that you can identify possible hackers. The code inspection system has been activated. Anything unusual will come to you for analysis. You'll be able to block codes to deactivate any malware. As you know, every operation is recorded in the database. It's mainly needed as proof when prosecuting hackers. You don't have access to the IPSs. If there's any intrusion, Security will get in touch with you. The systems are extremely efficient and make up for ninety-eight percent of human error. The other two percent is why we're here.'

Carda demonstrated how to open the access windows. He showed Vera each part of the intricate system which supported *Vatican World Cf*. 'The basic checks are essential in order to verify that it's working properly. You'll find all the technical information in the documents with your name on. See you on-screen.'

Spending the afternoon with Carda, receiving his instructions, made the time she was not with Galo that much worse. Suddenly the solace of the morning seemed to have been instantly wiped out, just as Carda had wiped himself out from the cybernetic corridors of her new terminal. Although she had a new job independently of Carda, more than ever she was being asked not only to be part of the virtual world, but also to rule over its meanders of which she was now a guardian. When Carda left at last shutting the door behind him, Vera remained standing in the middle of the room. Motionless within a strange silence in which the memory of Carda's presence hung as a pervasive mark. She shut her eyes. Her breathing deepened, trying to renew the space around her. With the tempo of her rhythmic breathing, Vera would fly to the same place where from the convent bell tower nothing threatened her. There, without leaving the world behind, it became a different space for her. Without imagining it, without time, without surviving. Vera spent longer there each time she went until she rid herself of the blunt ways of reality.

On hearing the shrill sweep of the magnetic card, Galo switched to the music station. Vera had just got home. She was not interested in commercial news, or political broadcasts, or advertisements for digital products. All predictable and interminable. Galo felt guilty when he followed the news that was repeated on *The Other One*, the only radio station that survived free of advertisements or commercial news. Like the rest of the population, Vera had a vague notion of the recent deaths. In a puzzling coincidence, suicides were being announced from various countries around the world on the few underground channel networks. The smaller voices of *The Other One* were lost in the powerful swirl of the political leisure markets. The minority group of listeners licked their lips in their obsession with opposing doctrines, devoting their free time to dissent. Microscopic within the megalomaniac technological system which worked flawlessly, their presence was barely an amusing sideline. *The Other One* broadcast the news discarded by the H.T. mechanisms. News that was scorned for not carrying progress forward, promoting well-being or stimulating the population. Vera was right. Life was to be found elsewhere, while Galo needed to fill his when he was not with her.

Life had not become any easier for Vera either. As Head of Updates, although he was not her boss, Carda continued to keep a close eye on her. They both reported to Zillo. At least it was not Carda she had to submit her weekly report to. Most of their meetings were on-screen, a constant reminder that he was sitting only a couple of metres away from her desk divided by a thin wall, which might as well have been invisible.

The new routine was merciless with Vera and Galo's dreams. These began to crack, separating the two of them in a deep, insurmountable dullness. The edge of the abyss was where they were able to come together again. They had almost become a couple like any other. Without embracing the interests of the rest of the population, everyday life seemed alien. They had to make an effort to fill the daily distance between them. Galo coped better than Vera. He found support in the reality he understood. Vera's reality was as intangible as it was shunned by others. Routine filled both of them with despair when the only incentive was to pass the time.

'Tell me. Show me where you've been.'

'There isn't much left to explore,' it pained her to confirm the presence of new barriers. 'Leave the music on. I'm exhausted.'

'Do you want to hold my hand while you sleep?' Vera closed her eyes and took his hand while she travelled once more far from her body. Galo held her fingers tightly by his side with his eyes open to the darkness.

The world was getting smaller, confined within stringent limits. Spaces fenced in by statutes, security, cameras, surveys, declared dangers, canonized procedures. Behaviour and routine all marked out. Clear boundaries against free will, desires, drawn like rails for the human soul.

Living was the only purpose of life. Existence reduced to its own defence. The planet as a museum of itself, its treasures kept as if in a national library. For those few interested, assets could be visited day in, day out by heliplane or by bus, along platforms as if on a conveyor belt. As though flicking through the pages of the planet wearing cotton gloves. For most people, from their screens – landscapes copied to perfection in three dimensions. With the holographic capabilities of technology. The planet with a higher definition than reality itself. A world duplicated on millions of screens to be visited by millions of avatars. 'For life itself' was the sole objective. Life for life's sake, the World Government had concluded, was the basis of society. There should be no other aim. The task was complex enough as it was.

Whilst Vera had been born against all odds, the alignment of the planets could not have been more harmonious. Easy aspects prevailed without any tension between them at the time of her birth. They revealed night and day, consciousness and unconsciousness. Nothing submerged or shut away. Emotions and needs out in the open. An exceptional awareness. Something which should make life easy and lucky for her. The extraordinary combinations and coincidences matched to produce an astral chart that was one in a million. Like tossing fifty coins and all of them falling the same way up. Heads or tails. She did not feel lucky that afternoon when she got home and found Galo hanging from a rope. Almost motionless were it not for the slight rhythmic swinging of his lifeless body.

They took magnetic prints and video. The police removed the body and left Vera with the care assistant, who explained the procedure and noted her wishes regarding the disposal of the remains. Just as he knew her in every feature, each gesture, Vera also knew that Galo would have wanted it to be her who gave him that final embrace. Before the officers, the experts, the assistants, the forensic scientist and their procedures. Before they processed the death of the beloved body. She climbed onto the trunk into which they had thrown the games. Galo had dragged it to the window in order to reach the beam which had served as a support for the final jump. When Vera cut the rope, Galo's body slipped gently into her arms. Sitting on the trunk, Galo lain across her lap resembled Christ in the painting in the convent's sacristy, the red cloth now covering his face.

Like Vera, Galo had no close family. Millions of people of their generation had lost parents and relatives. Galo did not know whether his father had left him at the orphanage having lost heart on losing Galo's mother, or because he had wanted to move on in order to leave behind a place he needed to forget. All Galo knew was that his father had never again got in touch. Vera could easily have found him on the Mother Hub. She had suggested this to Galo on several occasions. Although he had hundreds of questions, Galo did not dare to ask. Vera could not understand him. She herself was very curious about who her father was. She had asked Benedita, who had briefly talked to her about her mother. Benedita had drawn out the conversations, broadening what little she knew so that Vera would have a positive image of her mother. She dressed up what seemed dubious and responded evasively about what might be murky. She tried hard to make happy moments of their sporadic conversations on the subject of Vera's mother and was always ready when questions came up unexpectedly. On the other hand, Vera had interrogated her in vain about her father. It was as if he had never existed. Although perhaps he was around somewhere, as alive as she was.

Galo could hardly remember his father's face. He chose to leave him lost in the Mother Hub. What would be the point of finding him now, Vera asked herself, to announce to him that his son had died. Vera was certain of that and of one other thing. She knew where to spread Galo's ashes, although they had never talked about this, hoping that, by ignoring the subject, it would never happen. Those two certainties gave her peace to organise what she could no longer postpone. For the time being she had to put her feelings aside to attend to police, funerary and administrative procedures. The three customer care assistants of each of the departments helped her deal with the bureaucracy. She found it difficult to get rid of the personal care assistant, who pursued Vera for hours each day prior to the cremation, determined to ensure that Vera would overcome the loss. She had been specially trained. Vera's age group was assigned special services, whether Vera liked it or not. She belonged to the group of women under thirty-five of child-bearing age. She deserved a new opportunity to start a family, whether she wanted to or not. Vera was also in a preferential subgroup, having never given birth.

'Our priority is you,' the care assistant insisted. 'We're here to make the process easier for you. Reintegration into normal life. My job is to listen to you, understand you, heal you. If you need somebody to talk to, I'll arrange it.'

Proposals to organise her future for her forced Vera to face a reality from which she and Galo had decided to abstain. They had deliberately tried to avoid a life of conditioning. For her part, the woman made a real effort to follow the stages described in her instruction manual, while Vera wanted to tell her that it was not what she wanted. There were times when it was pointless to say anything.

'You haven't had any children. I'm so sorry. You mustn't despair. You'll have them soon. We will run a fertility test when you're ready. We'll call you so that you don't have to worry about it. Once you have someone in your life again you can go on the fertilization scheme right away. If you don't find someone within a year, we can also help you. You know there are other options.'

The assistant was there with her team to help her do what could not be put off any longer.

The safety guarantees took care of a world that was weakened in terms of numbers and birth rates. Studies showed a systemic fragility that needed addressing. It was not just that the sperm count had been reduced to less than half. Tests showed that only half of those counted were actually alive. Of those, only ten percent swam forwards. Ninety percent of the sperm of the post-cataclysm male population swam backwards. The tiny, invaluable cells were refusing to collaborate with the World Government's plan to increase the population. It had become as difficult a task as the forgotten pre-cataclysmic need to reduce it.

New methods of fertilization arose and with them the creation of a new field of employment.

Selection was rigorous. The condition was that employees should subject themselves to a strict health plan. They were monitored weekly. The 'super sperm suppliers' achieved sperm counts of almost thirty million, their work recognised as the new priesthood. They represented the statistical and true possibility of avoiding the progressive extinction of the human species.

Vera set off early on her bicycle with the urn in her backpack. It was Saturday. Not surprisingly, the streets were empty. She really wished she could see people on their way somewhere. She would have preferred it to have been a dull day, but the sun shone making stark the desolation of a land unnoticed, deprived of desire. She felt the warning of the cameras as she passed them. The only sound seemed to come from the oiled bicycle chain as it turned and the CCTV cameras which followed her one after the other as in a relay race. As if Vera were the only living thing defying the day. The only moving body. On a morning of special games on the national network around her there was nothing but diaphanous souls, thought Vera. She was not worried about the cameras. Neither did she approve of them recording her grief. She had jumped the perimeter fence. What an irony that Galo should jump with her, on her back. At least he would not have to answer if she were asked to explain herself. Once on the other side she lifted her arms in front of the cameras. What would they do to her: execute her for having chosen a place that was meaningful? For wanting to muddy her feet? Of course not. Those were words from the past. They existed solely in relation to the avatars who preferred historical games. The only executions were commercial or political ones. The only bullets, economic or public bans.

There she was, with an urn full of ashes, facing the unacceptable. Galo's living flesh had been transformed. His look and his skin, the external proof of his presence were simply impossible to hold on to except through memory. Vera's humanity felt more frail than ever, with her knees firmly planted on the ground she so loved.

She said goodbye to Galo in the same place where they had sensed each other for the first time. Lark's Wood, they had called it. Where Vera had predicted he would be and had gone to find him. There was not much left of the wood where Galo had become lost. The perimeter had advanced more and more until it almost reached the space surrounding the lake. As if the wood were an island, surrounded by turbines scaring off the birds. Galo and Vera had returned again and again, even though it saddened them. Even if it were reduced to a single tree where they could sit and be themselves. It was the only place they felt belonged to them. If Vera left his ashes there at the foot of the tree on which they had carved their names, a lark would fly to it. To find him, so that Galo would no longer fear the woods. She sat down where they used to sit with the urn on the ground between her feet. She unscrewed the top and leant against the trunk, resting her head on her knees. Her mind was emptied of all thought. But she had not risen to a state of abstraction which might bring her peace. Her senses were dulled. Without any will. Her spirit anaesthetised. She felt nothing but a void. The moment she had chosen to say goodbye did not come. Her only sense was of a desert in the middle of the constant whirring of the turbines. Then Vera looked up. The sound had stopped completely. She stood up and turned around. Not a single wind turbine was moving. They had all stilled. After a few seconds of total silence the timid sounds of the wood came alive, one by one. She looked down at her feet as if she could share that unique moment with Galo in the urn. This was the moment. As Vera finished spreading the ashes at the foot of the tree, she barely had time to offer him the thoughts that were starting to form. It was the unmistakable flapping of wings that made her look up. There it was, alone as usual, outside its habitat; keeping them company before flying to the plains where the grain was. The lark which always came to the wood while they were there. From the lowest branch it hopped to the base of the tree. The lark. In an embrace as real as it was incorporeal, Vera wrapped her arms around the tree, her heart pounding.

With her eyes on the rays of light which fell on her through the leafy treetop, she screamed just once, with the impotence of being unable to rise beyond. Of not being able, like so many times previously, to leave her body and travel. Even if only for a moment. To touch Galo on impulse.

That morning during prayers in the chapel, Benedita suddenly lifted her bowed head and opened her eyes, as if she had heard Vera's distant voice. It had been years since Vera's last visit. Years since she herself had last been outside the convent. Not since the Mother Superior had died. With the scarcity of novitiates, it fell on her to take on additional tasks. There were only eight nuns left at the convent. Through the years, Vera and Benedita had exchanged a few messages through her friend Dugati. The newspaper no longer existed. Nobody needed it any more. Information was available online where most of life took place. Dugati now worked at the Digital Information Centre. Not only did he agree to meet her and record the video message for Vera, he also helped her wrap the box and he himself ensured that it was sent. After so many years of seclusion, Benedita made the effort to go out, though not far. The time had come.

She had sent Vera a holographic message from the whole community. When Vera touched the membrane and saw Benedita's placid face crystallise before her, she felt a peace that would later vanish as suddenly as it had arrived. Benedita still had the same smile but she had either aged unexpectedly or they had simply been out of touch for too long. The distance had become even greater. Neither of them had believed it would happen although everyone feared it might. Benedita had never forgotten the tight embrace of her protégé when she arrived each day from technical school. Vera's absence had left her in a kind of limbo which she could almost remember in her bones. If Vera could not understand what had led Galo to such despair, neither did she have any explanation as to why Benedita had not come to see her. Instead she had sent her a box which would plunge her into much deeper confusion. It had arrived that morning when Carda's harshness seemed less tangible.

'Go home after the cremation. You have a week's break,' Carda had given her the electronic voucher. 'It's been assigned to you for your loss. I managed to book you three days in the Borneo reserve. It's the most exclusive one. No-one will disturb you there.'

Vera left the voucher next to the box on the table. The COS (certificate of security) label said it came from the convent. When she opened the plastic wrapping she found an old, yellowed shoebox. She instantly recognised the handwriting. 'My dear, you will think this is not a good time to send you this treasure, which you won't think of as such. In time you'll come to understand. Your Benedita.' The box did not even have a lid. Like the fine veil which had barely covered her head when she was born, the note served as a lid for a box of unfathomable surprises. With delicate fingers as if unwrapping priceless archaeological pieces, Vera lifted out one by one the objects she had been left by her mother. First the protective rubber helmet. Then the little vase, the candle, the figure of Saint Genevieve and the polaroid photo. Vera left the notebook at the bottom. She pulled the chair away and sat in front of the photo which she propped up against the rubber helmet. There she sat for hours until she fell asleep. With her arms for a pillow, in front of the photograph of her pregnant mother which she was seeing for the first time. From looking at her so long, she thought she felt on her head her mother's hand resting gently over the bump that was her.

She closed the notebook as if drawing a curtain over indecency. When Vera learned from the notebook who her father was, repulsion was her initial reaction. For her own body, almost. The idea that her flesh was part of that man. Her first thought was for her mother, whom she could not remember. Imagining her torment shook her out of herself.

Her limbs went numb. Her head felt the size of a pin, almost non-existent and at the same time a ubiquitous presence. She skipped from one thought to another, as if her head had been thrown into a pinball machine. The awareness of all those facts engaged with her more immediate reality. Galo had killed himself? It weighed on her like a responsibility that had never been hers. They had each decided not to live. The one who had given life to her, and the other who had been her companion in life. There was some sign of responsibility or destiny in it. She asked herself why she had been born. Why is each person born. The end of the road came so easily. With no preparation. Almost without thinking. The purpose of being alive could not be the contaminated world. The new electronic world. The vast machinery organised for the organisation of life. With no purpose – the purpose was organisation itself. The idea was frightening. Perhaps that was what had pushed Galo and Alina to the limit. Could she hold it against them? In the desolation of the field littered with dead bodies just like her mother almost three decades earlier, she could do nothing but weep. It was not from her own loneliness but the realisation of those whom she loved.

Perhaps time had not passed as quickly as Galo had hoped. The hours without Vera had become intolerable. Perhaps he could not cope with Vera coming home at night and sitting at the window in the moonlight. She had always gazed up at the moon. At times it seemed as if it was the moon who was watching her. As a child she used to ask it for things. Sometimes those things she asked for actually happened. Although she wished that Galo would come back, she knew that this time the moon would not please her. Vera sat gazing at the moon for longer than ever. She did not know whether it was her need to see it that made her unable to sleep, or if looking at it was what kept her awake. She felt no despair. It filled part of the empty void that overnight had been created by Galo's absence. Now her dreams had also disappeared, and with them, her capacity to control them. She had been able to decide each night what she would dream. Vera had flown each night creating her own dreamworld, since she had no way of changing the real world which surrounded her. Now she could not even remember her dreams. Just like her mother, a mysterious internal darkness had taken her over.

She got out of bed, her mind blank. She slept longer each time. Waking up to the surprise of still being in the world was more unexpected than the darkness of sleep. Galo had taken his own life? Her presence had not been strong enough. Nor had the universe they shared, full of meanings, of coincidences. What if he had not accepted the change of his schedule? Had his life been so delicately balanced that its preservation rested on this small change? The clarity which had always characterised her became fog. Although it was possible... Galo was not that straightforward. However many questions she tried to answer, what was mortifying her would not go away. She did not know what had disturbed him so much to deny himself and deny her and thus eliminate the cause. Of what? There was a veiled depth that however hard she looked would not become any clearer. For the first time the silence around her suspended her among inner voices.

She took the hand control which Galo had used to break that silence. With her thumb she stroked the keys Galo had pressed. Almost as though he were telling her to, she pressed the On button. The display in front of her revealed the latest login. The frequency he had been listening to that very day. It also showed the time. The difference between that and the time of death reported by the forensic scientist was minimal.

Had Galo had the forethought to switch off the station? Before killing himself? He had thought of her. Protected her against the cacophony of words, the voices Vera dispensed with. And his inert body? The atrocity of the surprise. The imprint of death on his pupils. Was it not necessary for him to protect her against that second in which blood freezes? Galo knew that rigor mortis would not shake her. The initial surprise would gradually turn into acceptance. The latter into understanding and then into harmony. Death for Vera was a stage in life. What would take time was the longing once she had understood the reason behind that act of violence.

In a reflex action Vera switched off the station. The voice of *The Other One* was cut off after a string of phrases from the news. She stared at the control in her hand. With the words resonating like an inner echo: 'wave of suicides… the wave of suicides…suicides'. She pressed On again and let the voices speak while she held her head in her hands and absorbed the news. Minutes, perhaps hours passed in this way.

Vera did not want to let the alien world permeate hers. Now she spent hours hearing about things Galo knew. '… reporting the true figures… shot up by 30%… lists online… the fluoridation of the water… lithium… liability… register it online…'

It was clear that the alarmist statements made by *The Other One* concerning the water were not the key to the suicides. Since the World Government had increased fluoridation and inoculation levels, Galo had installed an illegal filter. Water in all its stages was in the hands of the World Government. From collection, treatment and supply, to consumption. It was decreed that water was the most valuable of all goods for the human species. It was also the most strictly controlled, not only as a defence against past dangers, but for future prosperity. The eugenics programme inoculated water with nanotechnological vaccines for people's neuroprotection. Labelled by the World Government as daily 'food', they were delivered to every home without charge in the crystal clear drinking water. They provided immunisation against basic bacterial and viral diseases, including some types of cancer, as well as immunization against anxiety, anger, drug addiction. 'Cognitive enhancement accessible to all for work and play', the giant screens repeated endlessly.

She looked at the empty chair. It was where Galo sat when preparing lessons on the membrane. The image of the chair became muddled in random flashes. Vera did not know where the images came from. They were unconnected to each other, repetitive, as when, as a child, Galo's image came to her and drew her into the woods. In that boundless afternoon after which they would never be separated. Once again her visions took her to him. What did not make sense were the interspersed images. The empty chairs at two terminals in the processing room resurfaced in her memory as if they were the same chair. It was impossible not to notice the space among the hundreds of closely aligned terminals. She had seen them from Zillo's office at the last weekly meeting.

Her days were now spent allowing herself to be flooded by meanings brought to her by the death of both Galo and her mother; those that concerned their personal life histories. Although it was impossible for her to understand what those lives or those deaths carried with them, Vera did not want the path she chose to depend on eventualities. If there was anything she needed to understand, she would do so with all her senses. And with the awareness of that self which she strove to preserve.

Being alone had never been a problem for her. This time her thoughts linked together to chain her within the deepest kind of loneliness. They conspired to bring long forgotten mistakes to the surface. The present would reinterpret decisions made in what was now painfully obviously a past life. Galo and Vera would be no more. In hindsight, the right decisions of the past were now the cause of her misfortune. One decision above all now settled on her conscience with piercing insistence. It appeared to her as an unbearable mistake. When Vera had learnt she was pregnant, thoughts of her mother would not leave her. She could not chase away the comparisons that kept coming to mind. Her mother had given birth to her, even when she had been raped. Alina had never doubted. Without being paradoxical, her pregnancy with Vera had rescued her. The scarce days of her youth had been filled with a reason. Although she had not known it, the herculean task of saving Vera had been placed in her hands.

Vera, on the other hand, had been blessed with a good life like very few others. Now her secret had become a burden unshared; the meaning of her secret abominable, given the lives she had lost. Vera screamed in her dark bed. The child she had not wanted to bring into this world. The world she found so abhorrent had defeated her. It mocked her contempt. So it was not good enough for a child of hers? Neither would it be for her own existence, withdrawn from the reality into which she had been delivered. Even if she did not want that child, the world needed it.

Not long after they had moved together, Galo and Vera had conceived without any help from the fertilization scheme. The weight Vera felt now having lost a baby was not on her conscience. It was having missed the possibility of holding on to Galo through his child; Galo who had been as fortunate as she was. He had left her on her own. He had left her with nothing.

She recalled her initial surprise at the proof of her pregnancy between her fingers. The result: positive. Without any reservations, a new life was germinating. Galo and Vera had looked at each other differently with a look that was free of the conscience of the world. That night they had held each other in a tight embrace as though wanting to merge into each other's bodies. As though trying to remake matter for a complete fusion of what they were made of. As if it were a miracle. They were going to have a baby. In repeating that idea it began to take on other meanings. Leaving their surprise in the past. Spoiling the excitement little by little. They were going to have a baby. Each reiteration dispelled the magic a little more like a fine cloud. With each minute that passed, conscience invaded more of their space. Taking over the place held by the initial instinct. Vera, who saw things clearly, could only see a murky hole where the future seemed to close in. That was almost like giving up her own child to other voices, other plans. They would be expectant with predatory yearning. The ranks of technology at the service of science. They would be testing her -like the tests her mother had told her about in those brief lines in her notebook- this time to discover the secret of life. Galo and Vera were joint creators of a wonder, spontaneous fertilization an amazing event worthy of analysis. However hard she tried, Vera could not imagine any other future. She had infected Galo with the certainty of her predictions. Galo, who had resisted, allowed himself to be persuaded, in spite of his intuition for life telling him the opposite. Together they had decided to give up the miracle. The deeper significance would not be revealed until the end.

If the Department of Health were to find out, they would lose everything. It was no longer possible to get RU-486 at every chemist. It was strictly delivered under supervision by the Ministry of the Interior to very few clinics. The unauthorised use of the drug merited the harshest punishment. Exceptionally the authorities went with individual cases of a request for abortion. Galo and Vera had evaded the bureaucracy which would have denied them a termination of pregnancy. Galo had at last managed to buy the pill. It had taken him an unexpectedly long time. Between innumerable false trails, bogus online traffickers and the danger of the authorities breathing down his neck. By the time Galo found a reliable source, nine weeks had passed. Vera's physical reaction was violent and painful. The emotional cost was greater than they had imagined. Galo's fear had been of losing Vera. Now Vera had lost him.

She had once again survived. She was so like her mother, whom she sensed more than ever. She had seen the world like a factory, uninterested in life. She was right. So what? Her mother had given birth to her in the middle of death and despair. Vera's world could not be any worse than that one. Now she knew it was not. The world without Galo was worse than any other world. In the darkness of the living room, lying on the sofa, unable to enter the room where she had known such happiness, Vera was also somewhat like that uninterested world.

She had stood by doing nothing. She had not understood that Galo had a foot in each world. She regretted not being able to tell him. If only they had had the baby. Perhaps they would have been able to turn a new page. Days and nights became unusually long. In a second everything had changed. Her world had become as veiled as how she imagined her mother's had been. Vera had been abandoned by her moon. She put up no resistance to going through the terrible darkness brought by seeing the darkness of others. In order to understand one's own.

She allowed unknown shadows to touch her in the harsh desert where she suddenly found herself. During the first quarter of the moon she started to feel her muscles reviving. As if drop by drop the thaw cleansed her inside and out. She gradually opened her eyes to the silver light that was touching her once more. She opened out slowly to the nocturnal beams that entered the room to wake her from a journey from which she had to return. Her time had not yet come. She must return to shine in other spaces.

The electronic voucher Carda had given her was still on the table, next to the box she had been left by her mother. She picked it up and threw it into the trunk. The trip had expired but where she had been was far more exceptional and necessary. She put the notebook back in the bottom of the shoebox. She added each of the items in the order in which her mother had put them away. Her finger traced the image of her mother from her head to her feet before she put the photograph in the box too. She flattened each of the sides of the box to reduce the space and make a lid for it. Did the origin of her flesh matter? Did knowing it make any difference? She had spent her first few years in a convent surrounded by tenderness. Kind, generous women had nurtured her almost in silence. She had felt loved. She had felt no need to ask herself any questions. Now she had to be patient with the answers that would come in time. She might not have been able to bury her mother, but she could create a place to say goodbye to her. Her own place, where she would leave her little treasures. Next to Galo. As if keeping guard over them.

PART VI

All afternoon Vera tried to meet Carda in the corridors, the projection room, Cybersecurity, the control room, the entrance to the building. What she would not do was knock on his door. She passed it a dozen times and another dozen she opened hers just to poke her head out and wait for him to emerge. It was almost as if she were being made to pay for the times she had avoided him. If he was on-screen, he was in the building. She was just waiting for the moment to engineer a chance encounter. The day wore on without her having heard or seen him. Without being able to justify a minute longer of her allocated time, at the end of the afternoon Vera slowly went through the security checks, one by one. She closed her screen and prepared to leave the office. She opened the door once more. The silence as she went past Carda's office still denied her the possibility of an encounter. Once downstairs she approached the guard at reception.

'Have you seen Carda leave?'

The guard looked straight ahead as if he knew and did not want to tell her.

'Do you know if Carda's been by to…'

'Did you want to see me?' Carda's voice made her jump.

'No… of course. I haven't seen you today.'

'Shall we go?'

Vera walked alongside him, finding no excuse to chat. She clammed up and remained silent, as so often happened in his presence. When they got to the corner where they would go their separate ways, she managed to break the silence.

'Before leaving for Borneo I saw two empty terminals from Zillo's office. Another one this week.'

Carda stopped. Without changing direction, he barely turned his head.

'Yes, those vacancies have been filled. This week's will soon be filled too.

'Why did those operators leave?' Vera could not find a less direct way to ask.

'They usually change company. It's a regular problem we have.' Vera could not fail to notice the irritation in his voice. 'Cybersecurity have already checked the modular systems. There has been no leak of information.'

'Of course.' It was clear to Vera that this was none of her business. She lacked any pretext for further questioning.

'See you tomorrow.' Carda continued on his way, leaving Vera disconcerted.

If there was anything to be understood from the images bewildering her, it was clear that she shouldn't ask Carda anything regarding the company's employees, particularly given his odd answer to her question. Vera had not heard of any desertion of operators over the past few months. The zeal with which information was protected in the games industry did not give her any leeway to investigate.

There was no way she could get around the security checks, even if she could decipher the codes to access staff records. The measurement would alter the quantum system. It would be logged as an intrusion into areas she was not authorised to access. Vera had been born when security systems had failed. Like invisible wires fencing everything in, new mechanisms now flourished in a compact network of global intercommunication. At the same time as Vera's healthy nervous system was developing networks were filling in elusive spaces like swollen veins. Security services had unlimited access to citizens' data. From the millions of cameras to the databases. Security was a vast mattress on which big bosses slept peacefully thanks to the equilibrium among states. On the street, minor crimes had become sporadic events. Almost all of them acts of madness or recklessness. Anyone could become a suspect.

Cameras alerted security to any movement that strayed from predictable patterns of public behaviour. Sensors picked up noises in excess of certain decibels. The paranoia commonly felt in public spaces was not merely the result of intrusive cameras. A culture of mistrust had flourished after the cataclysm.

The commonest crime took place behind closed doors at a terminal. Cyber pirates used phishing sites to garner information. Stealing bank details and taking the identity of employees in order to access company information were severely punished. For many the punishment was no match for the enormous rewards offered. With PIX, the most advanced interception program, black boxes connected to the internet linked online information for analysis. Once on the mother server of each government, they interconnected with the Mother Hub. In spite of the high success rate of the cybernetic police, piratechnology was advancing in strides. It forced the Anti-Cybercrime Department to constantly keep one step ahead of malware creators in order to neutralise new forms of intrusion.

At the same time, analytical systems ensured employees' well-being. Employees were symbiotically linked to their terminals, every press on the keyboard monitored, its intensity measured through sensors recording the user's pulse, galvanic skin response, brain signals. Each facial expression was explored on-screen. The company offered support to tense or tired employees. It rewarded them if they were satisfied or, even, happy. Meanwhile each terminal logged the actual work done by an individual. More than ten percent of time lost was electronically deducted from their salary, dispensing with charts and bureaucracy. Working full time without any breaks was rewarded. Punishments or rewards did not interfere with the basis of working life. The hours of the short working day were easily outnumbered by those spent on leisure. There were generous incentives. Rewards were output directly to the terminals with the anticipated audio warning. The ping signalling a bonus was a welcome sound, similar to the buzzer used for the prizes awarded in games. The excitement of recompense for effort.

A daily quota for Internet access was a way for companies to avoid the need to block employees from using it at work. Once exceeded, daily access was automatically cut off. With each terminal opening on recognition of the operator's iris, the link between operator and terminal deepened, from their voice, to messages, replies. The terminal knew everything, gave everything, rewarded everything. It also demanded unconditional dedication.

With all websites registered on the Central Unit, control programs monitored any unusual activity. The cyber police would be aware of any breach. The world was a secure place. For the first time citizens were provided with the security they wanted for their leisure. With biometric cards, automatic recognition of number plates, identification sensors, location of mobiles, electronic travel cards – a fingerprint database at every airport in the world. Everybody was safe provided it was known who they were and where and how they lived, worked and played.

Vera waited for operator 324 outside the building. He worked at the terminal next to the one which had become vacant that week.

'Do you know his name?'

'His name, no. Some of his avatars. In *Cf* he's Conde90.'

'Do you ever play together?'

'We sometimes meet on-screen to compete. He's much more advanced than I am. No offence, but I prefer *Islamic World*. It's more user friendly. For him there's nothing better than *Cf*.'

'When did you last play against him?'

'The day before he left. I didn't see him on-screen anymore.'

'Do you know why he left?'

'I thought he liked it here.'

'Do you know where he lives?'

'No. Has he done something wrong?'

'Do you know 151 personally? He also left his terminal more than two weeks ago.'

'Conde90, and Roco55, that's 151. He was always on screen with *Cf*. I don't know his name.'

'What about 314? He also left.'

'Yes. He was in my column. I don't know him either. They were very advanced *Cf* players.'

'Do you know his avatar too?'

'Vals009. Now if you don't mind, I'm expected elsewhere. It's the on-screen *Street Marathon* tournament.'

Sparse as the information was, it revealed that the three operators were linked by their choice of entertainment and their decision to leave the company. She needed to find the common denominator. Though she did not know why she was seeking these answers like tiny pieces of a jigsaw puzzle, thousands of them, with Vera unable even to hazard a guess as to their final composition.

She stopped spending time at her natural refuges. In the morning she worked at home to find out where the three operators had disappeared to. It was not an easy task and it would take time. She only had the names of their avatars to start with. The sensitivity of the security systems meant that Vera had to tread very lightly indeed so as not to disturb a single particle which might give her away. The company would accept nothing but transparency. Although working blind, it was all she had.

Whatever their real names were, neither Roco55 nor Vals009 knew the operators at the terminals next to them. Neither operator 150 nor 152, nor 313 or 315 had a personal relationship, although they could almost touch the neighbouring operators. Their answers were even more laconic.

'Those colleagues are on-screen. We are linked by our avatars.' Operator 150 was more curt than 324 had been.

'I don't know those avatars. I hardly play *Cf.* I prefer games that aren't connected with work.' Operator 313 seemed to be a sensible person.

Operators 152 and 315 were more detached than the others.

'We're all the same, aren't we?' Was 152's only reply, after which he just stared blankly at Vera.

'I don't understand what you want to know.' 315 just turned around and left.

Games had annulled both memory and soul, which had become hazy through dedication to the virtual world. The soul was virtualised, mirroring the games. It reinvented itself with each version to overcome human limitations. In the games it seemed to achieve and gain it all. It would relate to other souls in nonexistent spheres. To burst like a bubble once offline. The simplicity of the moment was the greatest achievement.

Before going up to the flat Vera went into the self-service-meals zone on the west side of the car park with giant screens dominating each side of the vast square. The car park in the middle. Under the advertising displays, 3D screens ran whatever entertainment was on offer. Machines dispensed games, food, magazines, clothes. The streets were deserted at night. During the day, transport routes linked shopping centres. There was no window-shopping. The shops of the past had disappeared. Online ordering had gradually given way to the new business expansion. The self-service model. For food, clothes, medicines, daily essentials, vast self-service warehouses or a few stores had drive-through windows. Hundreds of products in dispensers were sorted by category.

Going for a walk on the streets was a thing of the pre-cataclysmic past; one went for a walk with the avatars in games. Only there did anyone make the effort to hike, run, climb mountains, swim in rivers, travel to new continents, new worlds, other galaxies, and fly. The freedom of the avatars was absolute. Thanks to technology, the pleasure of freedom knew no bounds. Avatars could be reinvented whenever and however people wanted. There was no need for them to be who they really were. Nobody controlled their most private desires, nor their most daring actions. Everything was possible. There was just one thing: in the depths of the hundreds of hours of their multiple different beings, despite the face and body chosen, in hundreds of miles covered, in repeated, new or invented experiences, in thousands of cybernetic stings, manoeuvres, crimes, heroic acts, each fantasy was registered under a real person's name with all the weight of identity for the sake of security.

She was assailed by bright lights, the uniform white tiles, like those of the morgue where she had touched Galo's cold body before letting the flames take over. Colossal refrigerated dispensers. Rows of heated cabinets. Thousands of cans of drinks and boxes of food neatly stacked behind thick glass. Cameras and sensors saw, detected, recorded everything. The unwelcoming feeling had prevented Vera and Galo from scanning their magnetic cards there on the way home, like everybody else, whether it was to buy daily hot meals, or frozen meals for the week. Instead, Vera and Galo would prepare meals from fresh produce they ordered online. Now she had stopped ordering it. Vera had more than one good reason to follow the general trend. She did not even read the labels of the *Gourmet Meals*. What Vera needed was a stack of boxes ready for quick suppers. Like everyone else. To minimise time spent away from the screen. Except that her purpose was different. She filled the empty freezer. She did not dwell on the strange taste. She needed all the time in the world. If only Galo could have seen her. After supper she would throw away the empty box, just like hundreds of thousands of operators who came home at the end of a day's work. Vera was becoming a member of the population.

She took Galo's membrane out of the cupboard. She had thought she would never use it again. At the bottom of the cupboard she found the laptop the nuns had given her for her graduation. At the time, state of the art.

Vera still remembered the Mother Superior's prolonged embrace. They both knew it would be the last time she showed her any affection. It had almost been the first. There had been no more celebrations, cakes, or songs. She could not recall seeing the Order gathered together ever again. It was probably one of the last times she had seen Benedita. She couldn't remember that either. What was now fresh in her mind like a thorn were the hours she had spent with Galo at the laptop. They had relied on it when creating innovative programs for their master's degrees. Twenty years later it could be found among the pieces on display at the Museum of Technology. Next to Galo's membrane the laptop seemed to belong to a different century. With a flick of the wrist she spread the membrane out. She gently touched the screen. It was the first time Vera had used Galo's PIN since his cremation. She had almost forgotten the welcome recording.

'Hello. While you work… don't forget the meaning.' Vera's voice framed by two beeps. Yes. What was it? Vera again touched the membrane, which switched to standby. Her deep breathing was just audible as she searched within herself. The previous weeks had shown her new ways of living, which she had not been aware of. She had always been wrapped up in her bubble of inner learning in contact with forces that the new order was bent on discounting. What if the world which nourished her were not the world she thought it was? She was alone and although this did not bother her, it had a bearing on a question she could not yet even identify. Perhaps a series of lesser questions would lead her to the big one. What was she looking for?

Why didn't she leave? She had planned to go off with Galo to somewhere where it would be possible to live differently, though they had no idea if such a place existed. Vera was not sure whether those were valid questions. Perhaps she only had one option left to her. To do what she knew best. To let her intuition take her wherever she had to go. Before opening her eyes she stretched out her hands until they touched the membrane. Once again with her eyes still shut she entered Galo's PIN. She waited until she heard her own voice and at the sound of the last beep, opened her eyes. She could almost see Galo's face in front of the membrane which he opened and closed like a child to hear Vera's voice during the long hours of separation.

After a few days Vera had become used to the food box routine. In the morning, sitting in front of the membrane, time fell away with the new ways she had found to fill it. The nights no longer felt so barren. She was no different from millions of others. She also isolated herself in her own territory. A minute spot to engage in. The cosmos of a person's life shared with a mere handful of people. She thought her rejection of a life which kept everyone happy to have been, at the very least, unfair. She began to understand the reason for the transformation of those souls. Their understandable choice when faced with the vastness of an unfathomable cosmic truth. Life was easy. The possibility of absorbing another reality practically nil.

She spent mornings and nights working. Nibbling at protein-rich biscuits and drinking tea in front of the membrane. With supreme calm Vera filled her resting hours content, as if Galo were there with her.

She knew the names of three avatars. To discover their identity, she first had to crack the password for each one. She would then have access to the online user account and their personal data. The first screen showed only basic details: name, date and place of birth, occupation. To get any further, she would have to crack the second password. The trickiest part would be breaking the quantum cryptography. Accessing all the user's information in the global database. Once inside, Vera would have to work fast. Cracking the second password would trigger the security systems. Following discovery of the intrusion, it would only be a matter of minutes before they located the terminal or membrane from which it had originated. Even if she got the second password, Vera would see nothing but meaningless symbols, letters and numbers. The information would be encrypted. Having none of the sophisticated blocking programs used by cyber-pirates to hand, Vera would have little time to deactivate the cryptographic security code. If she managed to restore the text to its original form and make it intelligible in time, she would safeguard her identity. Downloading the information would then take only a few seconds.

A month had passed since Galo's death when Vera managed to decipher the last of the three passwords for each avatar. After that long, tedious process, she was not going to be disheartened by the sight of unintelligible texts. But she started to have doubts once again. It was impossible to know whether she would find anything to justify the mission she had set herself. She was mentally exhausted. For days she had spent more than fourteen hours in front of the screen both at work and in the flat with the membrane. She went to bed knowing that the following morning would require even greater concentration. Although she would be facing the quickest stage, it would also be the most demanding. The difficulty of the task lay in constraint. Time. That morning, her mind refreshed and expecting to be almost at the end of the road, Vera set the chronometer. With an alarm every minute and, in the last minute, one every fifteen seconds. Five minutes was the maximum margin she should keep to in order to be sure of hiding her identity. She opened three windows on the membrane, one for each avatar. The first encrypted document she managed to decipher would enable her to crack the others more quickly. The code for each encryption would be the same for all files. She opened the first page for the first avatar. The chronometer began to run as soon as the second password opened the encrypted data on the membrane. The race against time had begun. At every alarm on the minute, she started to worry that five minutes would not be enough to decipher the code. With each alarm the pressure of time seeped through her skin in tiny droplets which she wiped away with her forearm. Without wanting to lose a second, the other hand continued actively trying, deducing, searching. Perhaps it would not be enough. She had done a few tests during her degree. Problem-solving capacity tests. Crypto-analysis for deciphering had not been a subject she had wanted to delve into. As if she could split the two hemispheres of her brain, Vera tested algorithms, sequences, while she dug into her memory for information that might be useful. Recalling data was not the problem. Rather, the question was whether she would find the solution among the things she had learned. By the time she was into the last minute, Vera had still not found a way in. She would not have another chance. If she exited and entered that user account once more, she risked the detection programs triangulating her location in seconds. Vera's typing speed was matched only by her skill at pinching and dragging contents on the membrane with her fingers. Closing and opening windows, activating and deactivating options, scrolling up and down lists. The visual delirium on Galo's mini-membrane was not born of chaos. On the contrary, it responded to a prodigious degree of concentration. The final fifteen seconds had begun when Vera tried one last possibility. At that moment she recalled Benedita crossing herself. She would look towards the ceiling as she made the sign with her right hand when it was imperative that something should happen, such as when Vera's permanence at the convent was at risk. Now Vera revisited in her mind each of the occasions she had seen Benedita cross herself. The last sequence. On her forehead, in the middle of her chest, to the left, to the right. Each of the movements of her hand coincided with each of the last five seconds. At the last second, with her fingers in the shape of a cross over her mouth, there it was. As though the sea opened up before her the membrane revealed the text and the images of the first operator. Clear, precise, beyond doubt. Nothing could be hidden from her now. On the sound of the final alarm, Vera hit Enter to download the document. Three seconds later she logged off, unscathed. Vera had become a hacker.

That afternoon she saw the faces of each of the three operators. She gazed at them, wanting to probe into the impassivity that contrasted with the zest for life displayed by their avatars. It was as if the essence of their real creators had been squeezed out of them. The bleep shook her out of her concentration, just when she was about to examine the data it had taken days to obtain. But the timed signal could not be ignored. Just a few minutes to get to work. She loaded the data onto her memory card. She rolled up the membrane and put it in the inner pocket of her coat. She grabbed the memory card and, with a protein biscuit in her mouth, slammed the door behind her. She got on her bicycle and pedalled off energetically.

She entered the Vatican Inc. building hoping nobody would stop her reaching her office to look at the data. Her weekly meeting would start in thirty minutes. She shut her office door. Once inside she did not insert the access card again. First, ensure that nobody can come in. Once in the office she must not compromise her usual behaviour. It must be just like any other day, performing routine movements for the cameras, positioned high up at both front corners of the ceiling, which ensured sufficient privacy for her to be able to open the documents from Galo's membrane. She could hide it from the cameras in front of her large screen. No movement should reveal anything unusual. Although it was forbidden to enter the building with membranes without inspection or authorisation, Vera had too many years' service to her name to be checked at the main entrance. The operators had to pass through the control side door. Where the analysing scanners could detect the tiniest chip.

She switched on her screen, which emitted the usual bleeps. Having muted the membrane, she rolled it out with the minimum movement possible. She sneezed at the same time as she opened it with a flick of the wrist. She began her usual activity on the large screen with her left hand. While following the personal information of the three avatars with her right. The cameras could not see anything. She did not even look up. Although she was more aware than ever of their presence above her.

The information showed the last job title and the company's name. IT operator at Vatican Inc. No subsequent job was recorded. She opened the second operator's window. There was no new company registered either. She knew the last one would be no different. Updates were done daily. If the operators had changed company, this would already appear in the records. It was an unlikely coincidence that the three would have decided to take a break at the same time. She knew it was also not feasible that they would have left together. They did not associate with each other outside of their on-screen avatars. It was as if they had vanished from working life. There had to be something else in the data. Something further to look for. Thousands of pages logged each *Cf* session. The user's setup, access to levels, duration, log-in and log-out times, scores, prizes, locations, power-ups, surprise options used, etc. More data about the participation or association of avatars in the game were logged than about their working or personal lives. It would take days to study the data, to find a mere hint. And what conclusion might she reach? What exactly had made them leave Vatican Inc.? At the same time as wanting to find the quickest way to research these questions, she knew she must not leave any trace in unusual places. She would think up an excuse to call them. Before leaving for the weekly meeting she copied their mobile numbers and addresses on her memory card. Almost without moving within the space occupied by her chair, she closed the membrane. She surreptitiously put the memory card and folded membrane back in her jacket pocket. There she left it, hanging on the back of her chair. She inserted the access card to open the door and left for Zillo's office.

'Carda said he'd be a few minutes late.'

Her new state of concern took Vera to the large windows to look out once more over the processing room. She noticed that the empty terminals had already been filled. At the back of the room there was a new asymmetry. At the other end, tiny, another newly emptied place. Far away, but obvious.

'We can begin with your report,' Zillo's hand on her shoulder froze her to the spot. 'You're distracted. It will take you a while to recover. Be strong and have faith. I hope you feel this house is your family. We're here to help you if you need it. You've spoken to your dear Benedita, I assume.'

Vera felt guilty. Her body reacted involuntarily, just like her mind.

'Yes, Father. I'm fine.'

'If anything's worrying you, you know you can come to me.'

'Yes, Father.'

'Something *is* worrying you. Am I wrong?'

'No.'

'Nothing which can't be fixed,' smiled Zillo. 'Tell me.'

'I was just curious, Father.'

She had embarked on weeks of research, many hours of her free time to investigate a simple absence of operators.

That was not her job. Nor did she have any reason to doubt the company. There was probably a simple explanation which Father Zillo could provide. It would then be clear to her. It was as absurd as it was senseless to blindly follow intuitions which had become superstitions. She was losing her common sense. And yet.

'Instead of your boss, think of me as an uncle or, given my age, a grandfather, if you like.'

Although Vera had the words on the tip of her tongue, different ones came out after a few seconds of silence during which Zillo waited with the patience of the confessor.

'For the next few days, could I come in in the mornings, Father? Have some flexibility?'

'Is that what's worrying you? Of course, my dear.' He took her by the hand. 'Of course we can arrange that. Whatever you want.'

'Thank you.'

'Only too glad to help.' Zillo touched the screen which showed the schedule for the day. 'Let's look into the GH3 mechanisms first.'

She made hardly any contribution to the meeting. With the growing number of *Cf* fans, Father Zillo was usually in an excellent mood when they met. If there was nothing pressing to deal with, after routine system checks by Vera and Carda, Father Zillo would hold forth as if philosophising were part of the agenda. It did not seem to bother him that neither Carda nor Vera expressed any opinion. Carda with his usual lack of expression. Vera absorbed in her own thoughts.

She could not wait to be back at her flat, sensing she was close to reaching a conclusion. Little by little her methodical steps were uncovering layers of information. The subscribers were not using their mobile numbers any more. The three operators no longer had a phone service. Another unlikely coincidence. Vera did not need to visit them to know that she would not find them at their homes.

The names of industrial spies appeared on general lists which were easily accessible to companies and the population at large, as well as being in internal documents circulated among the staff by Vatican Inc. She quickly verified that the names of the three operators were not on them. They had not disappeared due to any industrial breach.

It was clear to her where she had to look. It was just a matter of verifying her suspicions. While she sank her spoon into the contents of the *Gourmet* box, she read at speed to find the date and time of the last session of the avatars on *Cf*. It was as expected. The data of the past four months showed that they played regularly. Two or three times a day. Not a day had passed that they had not logged in to play, but by the end of four months the *Cf* session logs came to a sudden halt. This was another piece of information she verified without surprise. Once they had left their terminals at Vatican Inc., none of the three operators played again, either on their own against the machine, or in a group competing against each other. She knew that the next step was to look online. She took in details of the death of each one with little surprise: one had suffered multiple injuries with brain haemorrhage due to a fall from a height of fifteen metres. Another death: barbiturates overdose. The third, cause of death: external bleeding, slashed wrists.

The online lists published by *The Other One* confirmed that the operators who had left the processing room had killed themselves. Even though it was inevitable to her that Galo's name would appear on *The Other One*'s lists, seeing it among so many others shocked her.

The Other One blamed the world and its commercialisation of life. To preserve a world in control of itself. Entrenched in its precise, imperious vision of itself. 'We buy things with our eyes closed, it reported, seeing nothing but a thumbnail photo. Even if the product is unknown to us, the brand certifies its quality. Once we start on a series, we don't give it up. We buy in a chain: versions of a game, the next season's fashion in clothes, cosmetic trends, fashionable drugs, art, lunch boxes, membranes, electronics. The brand name is a sacred cow.' *The Other One* shouted to the world what everybody knew already. Only a few tuned in to listen. Only a few refused to participate in a market driven society. Life was made difficult for them but they continued to broadcast. They hoped for an unlikely awakening: 'We're survivors. Our descendents are as dead as the thousands of millions who fell in the times of terror. Don't let them alienate you from a life you don't understand. Governments continue putting human ingenuity to the service of killing off ingenuity. The protection technology affords you is not real. Government arguments recycle phrases to the same end. Life's proposal has been declined. Come to *The Other One* to hear the real truth.'

In spite of *The Other One*, the World Government had succeeded in achieving their goals: there were no debts to settle or crusades to defend. Humanity lived in freedom. Like a huge ball tied to an invisible chain, immaterial, unlimited. The chain of surveillance. *The Other One* asked ignominious questions from a dark basement: 'Is this what the population escaped death for? Is this what you are fated to be? What you should aspire to? Satisfaction from products one generation to the next. Developing the perfect product for the perfect action, the perfect result. Is your development the development of the product?' The voice emerged with all the depth of an invocation. While the few dissatisfied voices were easily dismissed as alarmist. It was natural that not everybody would be satisfied. Even if life were almost perfect, discontent was part of human nature. The World Government had an explanation. It was condescending and understanding. Everybody had a right to their opinion.

For Vera there was nothing natural about the disappearance of the operators. Carda's behaviour was even less so. He had told her they had probably gone to work for another company. Either the organisation had not notified the bosses or... Either Carda did not know that the operators were dead, or he knew something which she had to find out. *The Other One* was right. The intention was to hide the suicides which were increasing alarmingly. If Zillo knew about them, she could understand him refraining from mentioning them. He would not want to sound the alarm among hundreds of essential operators.

She felt a furtive satisfaction which was at odds with reality. There were others who shared her perception of life. Others also resisted being absorbed by the marketing maelstrom. Just like Galo, Vera spent hours listening to the news. Even if *The Other One* was right, she could not attribute those reasonings to Galo's suicide. She knew Galo's soul. Or not. Up to what point could she say so? Could she be so wrong about what she knew best? If she were, any certainty could vanish. The doubts that had taken her through dark paths had not been dissipated.

She restarted Galo's membrane with a nervousness that was new to her. She had to begin by systematically discarding one by one the possible answers, demonstrate that Galo had not been one of the despairing, 'empty souls with no essence', *The Other One* called them.

This time she worked in reverse order. She had the full name. To be able to access the data the variables were more predictable in following blocks of information on Galo to which she had access. The passwords were not difficult to discover. Vera quickly found the less intimate, although better hidden, information. Colder but burning. There it all was in thousands of pages. Vera began to browse quickly, as if jumping from block to block in her search. She read Galo's data as if she had not known him. Name, address, e-mail, profession, company, mobile phone, PEC number. Further on, each section detailed the person with whom she had lived almost since the beginning. She paused briefly at what had been registered before she knew him.

His family, his schooling, his medical history. There was so much she had not known. Details they had never talked about; he had polyps when he was two and then at the age of five had forced some seeds into his ears, which had begun to germinate. They had had all the time in the world and at the same time so little. What she now learned about him could fill a magical place where she could imagine him and make him present. She would leave that aside to later return to those moments and savour them. Vera scrolled down through the information on the membrane to reach recent data. Work, finances, medical, leisure.

When she saw the new name in the last section, she knew straightaway that it was an avatar. Neither Vera nor Galo had created avatars. Neither Vera nor Galo had ever played as users. Perhaps Galo had created it for work as an example and had left it there. Vera's wishful thinking ill-prepared her for the surprise. The login pages scrolled endlessly upwards and downwards. She opened them at speed on the membrane with her thumb and index finger while barely comprehending what was being revealed. There were hundreds of pages of daily sessions. The detailed log of hours of play. It was no different from the pages of the avatars she had investigated. Galo was one player more. His avatar: Lark.

She sat at the screen as if not caring that she only had a few seconds left before being traced. Although the alarm was screaming at her to exit, Vera could not hear anything other than the pulse at her temples. She went back to the first page to search for the games log. Only one was listed. Lark was registered for just a single game. *Vatican World Cf.* Vera saw the name repeated, mirrored to infinity. Despite her perplexity she managed to quickly download the file. In a reflex action she closed the membrane on zero seconds. She was left with a hissing in her ears in front of the flickering protector of the membrane. Once her discomfort lessened, the feeling of panic vanished. If she continued systematically she would get to the truth. She was convinced that the explanation would be so simple that she would later feel ashamed of having doubted Galo. Somebody must have used his identity. Identity theft for online avatars was not uncommon. Somebody who could not provide their own data to the system, perhaps due to problems with the law. Stuck in her seat, Vera reviewed the alternatives that would avoid that scenario. On the other side of her intense mental perseverance she found a long empty space. Conjectures were worthless. What she needed was proof.

As if propelled out of her imperfect serenity by a spring, she rushed to the trunk. Without exception, all the games had been buried there. Those that had come into the house as a promotion or company gift and had never been opened. She recalled the night they had dropped *Vatican World Cf* in like so many others. She reviewed it in slow motion: the box in the air, crashing onto the other unused packages. Then the lid of the trunk entombing it to lie forgotten under the red cloth. The cloth with which she had covered Galo until the police came. She rummaged frantically knowing that it should be at the top. Maybe it had slipped to the bottom of the pile. Vera was deluding herself. Not for long.

She rose from what she knew to be a vain search. She rushed into the room where she kept Galo's clothes still intact, as though he were to come home at any moment. Nothing had changed in the room where Vera no longer slept. She very seldom went in to fetch some garment or other. A place to enter and leave soon after. A limbo in which stopping meant letting herself be absorbed into an unfamiliar, lonely world. Everything in there could be transformed into an abyss where it is not possible to live. Rather than letting herself fall into it, she spun into an uncharacteristic frenzy. She pulled Galo's clothes out of the wardrobe and emptied the drawers all over the floor. She reclaimed the orderly, occupied spaces, to divest them of their meaning. Vera had lost her cool in a way that was exhausting. She emptied the walls of the photos of places they had visited together, memories hung as a window to the natural world. Places forbidden for their beauty. The room was no longer theirs. There was nothing she could recognise other than scattered bits and pieces spread around the floor, as if a gale had rushed through to void the memory.

Lastly, she climbed onto the chair where Galo would sit to work. There was one last shelf. Right at the top, reachable with a decisive effort. The shelf to which unneeded articles were relegated. At the back, in the dark, Vera's hand bumped into the box, recognisable by touch. So many times at work she had held it in her hand. This would not be the last time. Vera got down from the chair holding *Vatican World Cf*. She stared at it as if she had never seen it before. It had clearly been opened several times, too often. Galo had opened it time and again to remove the access key, glove, special control and projection card. Sitting on top of the pile of clothes, she held the *Cf* box as if she had found a bomb which had to be deactivated but did not have the strength to do so. There she remained, motionless on the floor without caring if the bomb might be about to go off.

The passage of time became evident only from the darkness of the room. When the pale moonlight became visible on her hands Vera stood up and switched on the lights. She went back to the membrane. The disappointment on seeing that stark information disintegrated as the idea came to her that it was not Galo who had experienced it all. The avatar which entered impossible situations was not remotely like the person Vera knew. It was easy to dissociate herself from the awareness that Galo had created that character. Now Vera had to find a reason for him doing so.

According to the records, Galo had logged into *Cf* every afternoon for four months. Five hours each time. From the moment when Vera had left for work until minutes before her arrival back home.

In the box she found the messages she had left him in his pockets over the time when they were not there for each other. The messages that had been written as a sign of understanding had become a poignant recrimination. The only antidote that took the sharpness away was the truth she had just discovered. Not only had Galo not visited the places which united them, he had lied to her. To seek a reason for this became increasingly urgent. He had not left a note. There was no sign at all. What could she remember of the day before his death? Perhaps Galo had been distant. Everything or nothing could be a hint of what was to come the following day. At best, it pointed to a tendency. It did not explain why.

If she looked at the events of the previous day, there was nothing but the strangeness of not being able to change anything that had already been consolidated in the past. Reality was made of different material than dreams where anything that one wished for could happen. She was annoyed when she realised that the material of which dreams are made was so similar to that of the games. She would think about that later.

Galo had taken any answers with him. He had not been enticed to play the new game out of curiosity but a certain despondency. He knew Vera would be deeply disappointed. He had no other way than to hide the afternoons he spent immersed in *Cf.* Like many others he spent his free time, the free space and its mechanisms, on games created to fill it. Vera had not been by his side to save him from that intricate, absorbing forest. Just like everyone else, he had become addicted to games. Galo only logged in to play *Cf.* What had become of the plans they had together? There had been only a month to go before they could start spending their mornings together again. Perhaps to begin a life elsewhere. She had no way of proving it but felt that there lay the key to what she wanted to know.

PART VII

On the following morning Vera knew she had to go straight into the inner workings of the game. She closed her office door and inserted the interface card. She opened the update file to access the mother program. The programming code she had written had not been changed. Neither was there anything unusual in the code within the sections programmed by Carda. The settings and the equations showed nothing untoward. Nor did the features or their variables. The node definition. Attributes. She checked the systems and particle formation, integrations. Inertia start-ups. Physical and mental response initiators. Sensory and magnetostatic convectors. All the sections of the game to which she had access were in order. To ensure confidentiality, the system would not let her access those sections with their password protection. If she tried to access areas for which she had no authorisation, she would be immediately found out. She had reached the end of the road. She must find another way. The only one that could lead her to the truth.

No matter how many twists and turns she took, she could not get to the solution. There was only one direct way. After weeks of research, there it was, staring her in the face. With no barriers, only danger ahead, she would follow the same route taken by Galo till the end. She would play *Vatican World Cf* every afternoon for hours. She would follow in his footsteps. She would try to find where he had become lost. With her senses sharpened she must seek in the game's virtual reality what she had not found in the mathematics and quantum science of its programming. Vera would have to become a 'games addict' as *The Other One* had named the population. 'The splendour of leisure' was the World Government's preferred term to refer to the games.

That afternoon when Vera went back to the flat something had changed. She had regained the balance she thought she had lost. She took a deep breath and exhaled sharply just as she would do before setting out to climb Monte Mario on her bike. To Galo, the views from the top were not spectacular but still the most pleasant of Rome. Vera opened the membrane. She registered her details under the same serial number as Galo's. A voice warned her: 'You are about to register the second user of your personal version of *Vatican World Cf*. Remember that this product will not be able to accept any more users. Please confirm the second registration or exit.' Vera confirmed the name Clarissa50.

Her work had become so automatic that she could barely remember the meticulous details of *Cf*. She had tested version *I*. She knew that *Cf* had far surpassed the original version. Vera personally had not incorporated any major changes in the programming, HUD or gameplay. The main difference she knew of was the huge number of fans who had been netted from *Islamic World*, *Earth in Peace* and *New Horizons*, the most widely accepted games of speculative strategy. *Cf* had also managed to keep its new and old followers in absolute percentage terms. Zillo had achieved what he had promised, with Carda's expert help. Vera had been instrumental in providing technical and scientific tools, giving expression to the design and some of the game's new elements. Now she would have the chance to experience herself what she had crafted using quantum theory.

She closed the curtain. Out of the box she took the glove Galo had worn so often in her absence. She inserted the card. There was Vera, before the magic of virtual reality in which she had so often declined to participate. She was no longer herself. Even if her avatar Clarissa had her same inquisitive glance reflected in her big eyes, in essence she felt she did not want Clarissa to be the same as her. She was supposed to be bolder, stronger, fearless. Fundamentally,

Clarissa should make no mistakes. The holographic projection took up the entire room. It invaded the space and made a new location of it. The vast virtual territory of *Vatican World Cf* where Vera or Clarissa or both now had to act. To change the circumstances which materialized, to avoid any mishaps, investigate clues, face challenges, seek the truth. Essentially, to survive. There were countless routes to choose from. Vera only cared about progressing through the levels as soon as possible, reaching the highest to where Galo had gone. Clarissa would take her where her own body could not go. If what had affected Galo and the others were there, Vera would have to explore it. She did not yet know how. But she would soon know if what she was seeking was only in her imagination.

The avatar Vera had launched in her place had the simplicity of a beginner. She did not want to overload Clarissa with gadgets she would later not know how to use. Clarissa's boots were no doubt special, like the ones Vera used to tread firmly in her natural world. The fewer gadgets Clarissa used, the more points she could accumulate. Courage was rewarded. Clarissa jumped from the shelf to St Peter's Square. She looked at her hands, torso, legs. She scanned her surroundings and smiled. She was ready. Before embarking on her task she turned to Vera so the two could look at and recognise each other. Vera had not stopped to think it over. She had chosen Clarissa's features in a hurry. The blond long hair, the dark eyes, the chalk white skin. Now face to face, Clarissa looked like Vera's negative image. Her long toned legs appeared to be the same, as well as her agility. One difference stood out. Clarissa had a demeanour Vera did not recognise in herself. Her avatar made her feel protected.

Vera had three weekend days before returning to the office. The goal: to conquer the fifth level and reach catharsis. First she recorded a short holographic message for Benedita. It was programmed so that she could deactivate it before the deadline on the day she went back to Vatican Inc. Otherwise it would be automatically sent once the deadline expired. 'Thanks for your message. I apologise for the time it's taken. If this message reaches you, it means I have killed myself like Galo. Not by my own will, but because of something I'm investigating which I might not be able to resolve. You must send this message with the attachment to the following parameters SON 6G 30313. They belong to *The Other One*, an underground radio station. Ask your friend for help. It's essential for the sake of the population. These years I have thought of you every day.'

Clarissa began to interact with the default characters. She was at level one. She was presented with a few easy questions and clear clues. She assessed the characters cautiously and accepted their company while she got to know the surroundings. The characters not only reacted to her own answers and questions, they also responded to emotional and physical information embodied by Clarissa within parameters which Vera transmitted through sensors in the control glove and by her facial response. Although it was all unexpected, the challenge had not yet begun. She would not gain anything if she acted cautiously. Her avatar seemed to be wandering around with no purpose. Vera was not taking on the challenge that Clarissa was designed to face. By looking at Clarissa's body language it was easy to realise that she had not been created for a menial existence. Vera knew she was wasting time. What could happen? That Clarissa would be sent back to the beginning and have to start again? The avatar's physical and spiritual death was not possible before reaching level five. The first challenge was to achieve a balance between precaution and skill to be able to make progress. To conquer in three days what hardened gaming addicts managed in two or three months. By the end of an hour she had activated a couple of characters on the list. The more characters she invited, the more complex the game would become and the more difficult the level. At the same time, if she did not activate new characters, she would not be able to gain access to higher levels. Vera went in ever deeper. Clarissa had already avoided being run over by a dustcart which had catapulted bags of rubbish straight at her. Following false directions from an ice cream seller she had lost herself in a labyrinth of alleyways crawling with gang members. After a punch-up with more than thirty of them she had managed to emerge unscathed from an attack by a rabid dog. She had then had to swim in the Tiber to recover the bag in which she kept her power-ups, stolen from under her nose while one of the newly activated characters was distracting her. On the first day Vera played for an unknown number of hours until she was suddenly overcome by exhaustion. She had pedalled, walked, run, swum, tripped, jumped. With Clarissa's legs she had covered miles without getting very far. Just a few seconds of carelessness were enough for Vera to lose concentration with unavoidable drowsiness. Clarissa dragged her feet to the end of the dark alleyway to lean back and fall asleep. Vera pressed the standby button and stretched out on the sofa until the following day.

'I have an ABD. Camera 16E detected anomalous behaviour in office 16.' Martino from Security approached with the memory card and inserted it into Zillo's personal screen. 'It has to go through you. She's management level.'

The image appeared immediately. Vera sitting in front of her screen.

'Do you take it to be conclusive?' Zillo kept calm without averting his eyes from the image of Vera.

'I'd say so. It doesn't show what kind of breach so I scanned and found the fragment.' With his finger on the screen, Martino fast forwarded the video a few minutes then pinching the image with his fingers he slid it to the right and zoomed in to reveal the metal plate on the lock system of her office door. As in a veiled mirror, it reflected a miniature image of Vera in her chair, seen from behind. In a minuscule section now magnified dozens of times it was possible to make out a characteristic brightness. The left margin of Galo's membrane.

'She has a membrane in front of her screen.' Martino stated the obvious.

'I don't suppose she requested authorisation.'

'No.'

Zillo's silence was unusual.

'This was not what came up in the ABD. I discovered it with the scanner once I studied the information,' continued Martino, knowing Zillo's weakness for Vera.

'What you're telling me is extremely important. Get to the point, please.'

Martino fast forwarded the recording to the end.

'The jacket.'

'What about it?' Zillo's expression changed from concern to confusion.

'She never hangs it on the back of the chair. I inserted the image in the search processor. Anomalous behaviour. In twenty years, she has never hung her jacket over the back of her chair.'

Zillo stared fixedly at the image for a few minutes until it became a dark background.

'I see. I'll take care of it. Leave the recording with me.'

Clarissa woke up to the fierce barking of a Doberman. The two Swiss guards watching her from above seemed gigantic. With her cup of tea next to her, Vera took small sips while she got over the shock. She remained alert to the dog's movements while Clarissa explained to the guards that she had fallen asleep. Vera had only lost a few points for her slip-up. Greater harm would come if she did not deal appropriately with the guards. Clarissa could not convince them of her innocent behaviour. These days nobody slept huddled against the thick walls of the Pope's office. How had she managed to get past the guards? Nobody could enter through St Damasus' Courtyard except the guards. She found herself sitting on the other side of the Vice-Commandant's desk. The questioning was not aggressive but became convoluted. The Vice-Commandant was a strict, inflexible man. How was it possible she had not been seen by the cameras or detected by the sensors? How had she managed to evade the chemical rays? Clarissa gave the wrong answers. If she revealed that she had deactivating devices embedded in her boots, they would confiscate them. She spent days locked up. Long minutes of Vera's real time. She needed an ally. Somebody who could help her overcome obstacles which made her waste time and prevented her from progressing. Vera pressed the Allies option. There were several dozen. She preferred to create one herself as a complement for Clarissa. If she generated her ally according to her own specifications, she would leave Clarissa almost defenceless. She would have to give up almost all the power-ups for that level. She had no alternative but to choose quickly among the default allies. It was Vido that Clarissa needed, a corrupt member of the Swiss Guard, even if she would have to drop him later. The priority was to get Clarissa out of the cell. Vido appeared with breakfast and a wink. When Clarissa saw the slight depression in the centre of the bowl of porridge, she knew she would soon be out. She savoured the last spoonful of porridge. With the additional taste of the magnetic key Vido had left in the viscous mush.

The familiar footsteps announced themselves in the Budbar. Sitting in his usual private corner Zillo kept his eyes fixed on the membrane on the table.

'It's no longer possible to read the alternative information. Several suicides and they're off, blathering on about the cataclysm again. Don't they realise they only scare people? As if they were capable of analysing anything. Did they not know that in classical antiquity they already had specialists who poisoned the drinking water? They infested besieged cities by throwing vessels with fluids of those sick with cholera or leprosy into the water. European settlers did the same thing. They annihilated native populations with flu, smallpox, typhoid fever, whatever. More powerful than steel or powder. The penny hasn't dropped that we still live in the same way. The main thing has always been to protect stability. Dominant groups will never give up their interests. The market cycle is unstoppable. It would lead to a worldwide catastrophe. Everything depends on everything else. Easy to succeed and equally easy to fail. It will always be the favourite game. Don't you agree?'

He waited for Carda to sit down before looking up.

'I imagine you have something pressing to discuss with me.' The priest's preambles were well known to Carda,

'I received notification from Security. An ABD.' His face indifferent, Carda said nothing. Zillo rubbed his temple. 'I hope it's nothing. They detected anomalous behaviour in Vera.'

Zillo inserted the card and turned the membrane.

'Look at all three files.' He again rubbed his temple while Carda studied the information.

'She smuggled in a membrane. I see. She used the jacket over the back of her chair to hide it. Her movement is barely noticeable. Deliberate concealment.'

'I asked Martino for more information before arranging to meet you.'

'Did he find anything else?'

Zillo touched the membrane to open the video and turned it again towards Carda.

'The external perimeter cameras show her waiting and then talking to two operators.'

In a few seconds, the video clearly showed Vera standing talking with operator 325. After a slight hesitation Vera leads him out of sight of the camera.

'Their terminals were next to the two operators recently departed.'

'Spying, Vera?' Carda's incredulous grimace did nothing to hide his cynicism.

'She's a little disoriented after her partner's death. They were together for many years. Martino looked into the business of the operators leaving. They had also killed themselves. The apparent wave of suicides is clearly worrying her. See what you think.'

'It all points to one conclusion. Why would she bring in a membrane?'

'She could have done so years ago. There is no record of invasion of restricted areas. So far I have no reason to suspect her of spying. Speak to her. Use my office. I don't want any cameras recording this situation. I don't wish to besmirch her reputation unnecessarily. Tell her what we have on her. Don't tell her I know. When you've clarified the issue I'll expect your report.'

Carda preferred not to speak to Vera. The first thing was to look into the register of her daily activity. Martino provided him with all the logs for the past four weeks showing each sector where Vera had worked and on what. The time spent. Steps followed. Websites she had visited. Zillo had given him complete freedom to investigate Vera. Martino had reluctantly given him her PEC number. With it, it did not take Carda long to rake through her whole life. He accessed the global database in the same way as Vera had illegally investigated the operators. Carda studied every fact about her, getting to know her tastes, her habits, her dislikes down to the last detail. He checked her out once more using the ABD. Two anomalous behaviours emerged, both in the past three weeks. For Carda the signs of Vera's intentions were conclusive. It was not the constant visits to *The Other One* that caught his attention. Vera, who had never registered a single avatar for any game, had embarked on a sudden daily routine, spending hours on *Vatican World Cf.* It was the definitive proof of what he had begun to suspect. He had such a clear profile of Vera that nothing could dissuade him or stir any doubts. For the first time in years, fully aware, Carda's lips broke into a smile.

Once at the third level, Vera had a more comprehensive idea of the marvellously complex world of *Vatican World Cf.* She did not know whether the desire to go further was hers or Clarissa's. The hours went by almost without interruption except to eat something she had allowed to go cold on the plate next to her. They were hours in which the surroundings changed at every corner and presented her with riddles, challenges she had to overcome to advance, not knowing where she was going. She spent the first two days with the curtains drawn, attempting to advance from level four to level five. Galo had spent his last few days there, increasing his score and prizes each time. According to Galo's logs, there was little room for improvement. He was an advanced player. He had conquered obstacles and reached catharsis three times. Just like the other dead avatars, Galo had reached the climax. Level five was the top. Vera had not imagined that the complexity of the game would make rising through the levels so laborious. She would not be an advanced player until she reached the fifth level.

Vido turned out to be a remarkable ally. Not only had he got Clarissa out of the cell, he had not hesitated to desert the Guard. Nor had Clarissa hesitated to take him with her. Thanks to his internal knowledge he had helped Vera climb sub-levels without her knowing it. Clarissa depended on him. They had become an efficient, devoted team. Meant for each other. Clarissa had also had to save him on a couple of occasions. She had jumped off a motorbike to prevent him crashing into a combi because his brakes had been severed. Even more dangerously, Clarissa had risked being demoted to the third level by her decision to retrace her steps to rescue him. She had yanked him out of the cage seconds before its walls were compressed or he would have been skewered by poisoned barbs. Each time Clarissa and Vido made a high five, Vera scored more points that would take her to the top.

He went into the Budbar, straight towards the private section at the back. Carda was waiting for him. As Zillo passed by, he gestured to the barman. By the time Zillo had removed his overcoat and hung it on the coat rack, the barman had appeared with two glasses of brandy. Zillo sat down opposite Carda.

'Who'd have thought it? It feels like it was centuries ago. The days we used to come to take our friends to parties in Rome. Another era. You can't even collect art now. It's pure exhibitionism. When the Chinese bubble burst, who was left? Until the next bubble. What do they know about art! Whatever happened to aesthetic excitement? Paris, London? Those were inspirational cities. Artists breathed the life of an era. Now they breathe the construction of a brand name. I'm leaving for Paris in an hour. Back in a couple of days. I'm leaving you in charge, *comme d'habitude*.'

It bothered Carda when Zillo displayed his good mood. He felt at a disadvantage. Zillo slipped him the access card, sliding it across the table with his palm face down. Carda waited for Zillo to lift his hand before taking the card. He raised his glass and gulped its contents down in one swig. Zillo raised his and peered at the bright amber liquid. He swirled the glass while covering it for a few seconds. Then he put his nose closer and took away his hand to inhale the brandy's powerful aroma.

'An excellent distillation. Colombard.'

The two men felt comfortable with Carda's silence. Zillo again sniffed the aroma of the drink several times after making the brandy swirl about gently in the glass.

'Very good. So, what do you have for me?'

Zillo pushed his full untouched glass away with the

back of his hand as though it were in his way. Carda put the memory card on the table. He pushed it gently towards Zillo with his finger.

Once he parted with Zillo outside the Budbar, Carda texted Vera asking her to meet him at Zillo's office. Vera was seated waiting at the conference table at the other end of the room from the glass wall. Carda came into Zillo's office and shut the door. That Carda should not reinsert the access card worried Vera. The tiny red light on the lock plate lit up. Forgetfulness or not, the door was locked. The curtains closed instantly when Carda pressed the button. Although Vera felt herself locked in Zillo's office, she hid her nervousness.

'And Father Zillo?' Vera knew the answer as Carda approached her.

'He won't be coming.'

Vera got up from her chair but his firm hand pressing on her shoulder told her clearly to sit down again.'

'We need to talk.'

She had never felt such unequivocal firmness. Carda had always seemed to her to be a weak man despite his harsh character and inflexible attitude. Vera resorted to her rhythmic breathing. Carda walked to the other end of the table.

'We know you didn't go to Borneo. Any reason why not?'

'I haven't been feeling well. I preferred to stay at home.'

'Understandable, but you lied. Any reason?'

'I didn't want to worry Zillo.'

'There are no cameras or microphones here. You know that.'

'Yes. I have nothing to hide.'

If they doubted her behaviour, why was Father Zillo not there to question it?

'The access logs show you have been checking the *Cf* structures.'

'I had reason to think that the gameplay might have been altered.'

'What kind of alterations?'

'That's what I wanted to check.'

'You didn't receive any alerts.'

'My job is not just…'

'I know full well what your job is.' Carda's harsh voice was nothing new. She had to keep calm to emerge intact from the interrogation. 'I also know what your job is not.'

Vera recognised instantly that this time Carda's silence indicated that he was expecting an explanation. She preferred not to offer any that could suggest her weakness on the topic.

'Martino has notified me of an ABD related to you.' Once Carda understood that he himself should continue the conversation, he inserted the card in Zillo's screen. In the heavy silence Vera began to speculate on possible answers. The enormous image of herself on the large screen shook her to the core. He showed her evidence of her infringement. The conversations with the plant operators and her jacket on the back of the chair, which had been the giveaway.

'Introducing a membrane without due authorisation is serious. Do you have a satisfactory explanation?'

'It was a mistake. I should have left it at home. I wanted to review Galo's documents.'

'At the office? Hiding it behind the screen? And your free time? I hope you can offer me a more convincing reason.'

Vera was practically telling the truth. She had underestimated the systems and they had worked against her. Clearly sticking to silence was the best thing to do at this time. Carda had no problem with his own silences. Vera took advantage of Carda's pause to resume her deep breathing.

'I have been asked for a report. I delivered it this morning.'

Her hands felt cold. She had been sitting for too long being analysed by a man who had always despised or resented her.

'I don't know what the report says but I'm glad. I prefer to explain it all to Father Zillo.'

'Explain what? That you're investigating the suicides of the operators? That you think they're linked to *Cf*? That it's the reason you play every day? To investigate what you haven't been able to here because of the security networks. I know every step you have been taking. What I can't understand is why you brought in your membrane if you knew it was not possible to connect it to the system.'

'If you know everything, why are you interrogating me? Why isn't Father Zillo here?'

Carda leant forward across the table. He rested both hands on the table with his arms stretched out. Carda's face was inches from Vera's as he held her gaze.

'Because I want to help you.'

The unknown frankness in the tone of his voice made her catch her breath. Her cold hands received a surge of heat. From her hands to her face, Vera felt the rush of blood reddening her cheeks.

As Carda's last statement resounded in Vera's incredulous ears, the Vatican's jet was taking off with a roar. Zillo inserted into the membrane the data card that Carda had given him in the bar. He used the armchair controls to communicate with the cockpit.

'I'll be busy for a few minutes. I don't want to be disturbed. Lunch in twenty, please.'

'Yes, Father.'

Zillo closed off communication and pressed Privacy. A few seconds after the cockpit door shut, Carda's image appeared on screen.

'The report is negative. The membrane Vera took into the building is her dead partner's. She opened it in my presence. Although there are no records of intrusion in the prevention system, I put the device through the IPS. Negative. On the day of the breach she had two of her partner's recordings open. She claimed personal reasons although she admits it was an error to have brought in the membrane. I used the SRDs. The interview revealed that she's in a fragile emotional state. She admitted using her jacket to keep the device hidden from the cameras. I checked all the logs. She has not incurred any further breaches. I also spoke to the operators she questioned. She wanted details of the relatives of the dead operators. They assume it's to share her loss. The operators interviewed had no relation with the deceased men. She has not spoken to them since. She has been seeing a personal care assistant. It's all above board. That's it. She's clean. I'll continue monitoring her closely but there's nothing else. Have a good flight.'

Zillo sent a message to Martino. 'Leave it with me. It's all under control.'

Still seated at the conference table, Vera held a distant, reserved expression, as if she had caught it off Carda. Once again her mind was being split between absorbing every word and processing the surprise that was unfolding. If Carda was not the person she had thought he was, he was the complete opposite to that person. He was someone towards whom suddenly she could feel a deep empathy.

'It's the game. I think there's something in *Cf* that disturbs or disorients. I've been analysing it since he asked me to investigate you. Obviously the suspicion against you is one of industrial espionage.'

Vera smiled at Carda for the first time.

'What else is there to live for?'

'Precisely. I have just presented Zillo with a report. It clears you. I've alluded to personal reasons. Nobody else knows of your offence. It's up to me to close the file on the investigation and it's now closed.' Vera could not get a word in. Carda did not expect her to. 'I don't know how it happens. When competing against the machine, neurokinetic behaviour is altered. I checked the kinetic logs of the suicidal operators.'

Vera lowered her head as though Carda had punched her. Surprisingly, Carda acknowledged her reaction.

'I'm sorry. I didn't realise.'

'Carry on.'

'I used the PECs and accessed the *Cf* logs. There's a void of both kinetic and emotional information when players reach the final stages of level five.'

'Yes. I noticed it too in Galo's logs.'

'It's the same information gathered by the sensory response detectors for each terminal. Even though the logs show that the players suffer a kind of neurokinetic paralysis they continue playing in spite of it. That shouldn't be possible but I've already checked and it's not an error in the logs.'

'Does it work like a hypnotic force?'

'Maybe. I'm not sure what it is, specifically. Nor what provokes it. I searched more than ten games used by those operators. There is nothing similar in them. It only happens in *Cf*.'

'I know. It doesn't make sense. We have almost three hundred million users. There have been fewer than one hundred thousand suicides.'

'*Cf* is relatively new. Not everyone reaches the top level. Remember that one of the attractions of this version is the difficulty in winning.'

'Not everybody reaches catharsis?'

'I don't think so.'

'If it's something in *Cf*, how and why?'

'Let's concentrate on how. There are areas I can't access, just like you. The code for some sectors was written at headquarters. Those sectors came from the United States and were installed later.'

'That I knew, and always wanted to ask you who installed them. Who wrote the code?'

'I don't know. As usual, the explanation I was given was "security". Zillo had never before excluded me from a sector.'

'Father Zillo?'

'Who else?'

'I don't believe it. We must talk to him.'

'Until we know what we're dealing with and who's involved, we can't exclude anyone or involve anybody else in the investigation. I trust you'll agree.'

Vera did not reply.

'I can imagine what you must be thinking,' added Carda, 'I don't blame you. I've not been a very friendly colleague.' Vera was not sure whether Carda had deliberately used a euphemism or whether he did not see himself as harshly as she did.

'I have to go briefly to my office.' Vera needed some time alone, even if it was a few minutes.

'We haven't much time. Zillo will be back in a couple of days. He gave me his access card.'

Even if this was a mistake, Vera had to take the chance. Suddenly she was not only trusting Carda, she was also committing to sharing her intuitions and fears with him. Vera was turning Carda into an ally.

Sitting in his hotel room in Paris, Zillo's face appeared on screen. On the membrane Carda's face, looked different from the image Zillo was used to.

'Looks like my absence has cheered you up. How's Vera?'

Carda hardened his features.

'She's recovering. I suggest you don't mention you're in the know.'

'Of course I won't. I don't want her to think I doubt her. Nor should she feel she's under observation.'

'That's right. I'll follow her behaviour closely. I've asked Martino to notify me immediately of any anomaly in the log.'

'Good.'

Carda managed to finish his conversation with Zillo long before Vera came back from her office. She had gone there to deactivate the holographic message she had addressed to Benedita. She put it in her pocket as a precaution. It would take her seconds to send it if events demanded it. Vera took a deep breath before going back into Zillo's office to meet Carda.

'I looked into it but it's not possible to access those sectors. Not even Zillo can get into them. Once installed, biometric security is linked up in columns. If we enter, Security will come down on us immediately.' Carda kept his eyes on the screen.

'What do you suggest?' Vera asked, already knowing what the next move would be.

'That we analyse Zillo's mail during the months *Cf* was being developed and any associated documents.'

Vera's wariness was not just because she was invading her mentor's privacy, she was feeling guilty because of her need to prove that Father Zillo was not involved in something unspeakable which she figured had led Galo and so many others to suicide.

'If there's anything to be found, it has to be here.' Carda, on the other hand, expressed a steely conviction. 'We need the passwords.'

'I think I can break them in less than half an hour.'

'I'd hoped as much. We mustn't work outside office hours or the ABD will be triggered.'

Carda inserted Zillo's card. He ushered Vera into his chair with what looked like a smile. The more friendly his recent behaviour, which Vera could not help comparing with the Carda she knew, the more she was assailed by doubt. According to the law of probabilities, for Vera such a change was inconceivable. She must carry on. She could not go back. If she refused to cooperate, she would make an enemy of Carda. If her doubts were unfounded, she would get to the truth with Carda's help. If they were justified, she would have to think how she could defend herself against the consequences. Vera could not even speculate what these might be nor why Carda had decided to take this new path. At that moment she could not afford the luxury of reflecting on a possible way out.

Vera had deciphered the access passwords sooner than both expected. While Carda checked the hundreds of documents associated with *Cf*, she looked for any revealing information in Zillo's mailbox. Unexpectedly she was making strides now that Carda was on her side. Vera was not sure whether he was helping her, or she him. The ambiguity of this collaboration did not prevent her from giving everything she had. At the end of a few hours neither of them had found anything to support their conjectures. On the one hand, Vera was glad not to find anything which implicated Zillo. On the other, she was still wondering what Carda wanted to find and why. It might not be the same thing as she was after.

Vera began to look for ways of avoiding collaboration with Carda. Time sped by. In less than an hour they would have to close the screen and leave the building. Her attention was divided once again. If she could convince Carda to interrupt the search until the next day, she could secretly contact Father Zillo. Warn him, although she was not sure of what. As she investigated his e-mails, Vera was plotting an about turn. She had stood up. She was ready to divert the investigation. At almost the precise instant when time and her will came to a standstill for a few seconds, her attention suddenly focused to zoom in on an element, isolating it as if under a magnifying glass. There it was, the sign. Even without the precision provided by an ABD, among the sea of e-mails to the usual recipients, one new name surfaced like a unique piece in the collection. Only two e-mails sent by Zillo to this address clearly represented something unusual. What was even more striking was what was missing. That the recipient had never replied was more significant than any documents they could be looking for. Vera analysed the details. She did not know the name nor was there sufficient information to decide whether or not it meant anything. She turned to Carda. Absorbed in fast-reading the documents, he went from one to another at speed. She recognised in his face the blank canvas of his expression. She would have given anything to have some insight into what she thought she had discovered without having to share it with Carda. However unique, an item of information was no use if it meant nothing to her if she was not equipped with the knowledge to give it value. She was bound to cooperate. Being unable to read either its essence or Carda's, Vera closed her eyes and decided to take a leap.

'Do you know a Daniel Lo?'

'Of course.' Carda's face changed. He got up immediately and went to Vera to peer at the screen. 'The great Daniel. He's an exceptional programmer. He was one of my teachers.'

'I thought I recognised the name,' Vera lied. 'There are two e-mails Father Zillo sent to Daniel Lo. There's no reply. One to arrange a meeting in the Budbar. Another to tell him about a bonus.'

'Bonus? Daniel retired years ago. What's the date on them?' Carda preferred not to mention the Budbar.

'The first meeting was some six months before the launch of *Cf*. The other was a week after the launch.'

Carda and Vera looked at each other for the first time with one certainty in common.

'I can trace his e-mail address and briefly access his PEF to get his details,' Vera continued not only revealing her skills as a hacker but also openly offering them.

'You can't do it from Zillo's screen.'

'I know.' Vera would have preferred to get the information without his help.

Even if she wanted to, there was no way of getting rid of him and continuing on her own. Her options were limited. To access the personal electronic files they had to do so either from her flat or from Carda's. The proposal was clear. She couldn't envisage Carda being in her flat where she had so often talked to Galo about the attitudes of her ex-boss. Now he was not only a peer, but a colleague. The second option was even less attractive. She was not used to making sudden decisions. Circumstances were demanding; even when they gave her vertigo, what Vera did not lack was boldness.

'Let's go to my flat. I've used Galo's membrane to access the PEFs. So far I've managed to evade being traced.'

'Perfect.'

Carda activated his sensor and copied the e-mails on the screen. He copied all the documents still to be examined onto Zillo's membrane and removed the card. He closed the screen, rolled up the membrane and put it in his pocket.

'I'm going to my office to check that everything is in order. You do the same and I'll meet you outside in twenty minutes. It's best if you leave first, in fifteen minutes. Walk to the corner and pretend to take a call. I'll catch up with you when I leave.'

Vera would have preferred them to leave together. Although there was enough justification not to, to avoid their exit being logged as anomalous behaviour. She could not make out if Carda was protecting the investigation, himself or, implausible though it might seem, her.

Vera inserted the access card in spite of a persistent feeling of disquiet. As soon as they arrived at her flat she hurried inside to check that the bedroom door was locked. This was the room she had left in the chaos of the other night, so brutally revealing. Carda was waiting in the corridor and it felt inconceivable to let him in. Now Vera must shut out any hesitation. She had nothing left to lose.

Once again silence hung between them on crossing the threshold of the profoundly private space. It was where Vera had lived most of her life with Galo. There where Galo had decided to strip her of his existence. Where Vera had discovered his body and his secret. Now she opened the door to a nameless new phase. Nothing in her experience was quite like this. After the initial wariness on feeling Carda's immediate presence, Vera discovered how and to what extent the past few weeks had transformed the space. The past hardly existed any more. Now more than ever it became a place for seeking the truth.

She gave herself a break after the initial shock, busying herself with the routine of defrosting two *Gourmet* boxes and putting them on the table. There was no need to invite him to sit down or share supper. Carda made the transition easy for her by keeping his distance. Responding to the clear non-verbal instructions of his reserved behaviour, Vera switched on the screen to fill the void with *The Other One*. In silence they stared at their food and like two animals cautious about their surroundings they ate unusually fast, eager to resume the investigation. Even if *The Other One* announced the most sensational events, Vera and Carda could only hear the shrillness of their own thoughts. Once freed from the need to recharge their batteries, the task in hand would bring everything back to normal.

Vera sat down with Galo's membrane. Carda continued looking through the *Cf* documents. Even though it might be risky, taking Zillo's membrane was the only way of getting classified information out of the building. The security systems would track the incompatibility of any other membrane or memory card. Security would sound the alarm.

Accessing the PEFs and downloading information had become routine for Vera. The task took her no more than a couple of hours. Finally Carda and Vera sat down to analyse the master programmer's personal, professional and financial information.

'Just as I said. Daniel's been retired from programming for years now. And from teaching.'

'There aren't any payments made by Vatican Software Inc. around the dates of Zillo's e-mail, either. His last income from the company was before he retired.'

'Daniel hasn't worked for years.'

'The bonus Zillo mentioned doesn't make sense.'

'Of course not. It's not even official. We'd better pay him a visit,' Carda took the initiative – and, for the first time, Vera did not feel threatened.

Perhaps Carda's harshness was related to his unconditional dedication to work. For years now nobody had kept him company, or waited for him, or mentioned his name. Everybody had at least one person even if it was just a friend or someone in the family. Carda seemed to be a man distanced from everyone. The only apparent link was with Zillo. A cold but familiar link. The familiarity of work. Although Carda's private solitude was an unknown quantity, it explained his curt behaviour better than anything else. Maybe it was just extreme awkwardness. Inexplicably Vera felt for the first time a certain clumsy warmth by his side.

They travelled in silence through Rome's neighbourhoods of new apartment blocks. When they arrived at the address, Carda rang the doorbell several times. They waited for Daniel Lo to answer. Nobody did. They hung around the door for someone to enter or leave the building. When a woman appeared, Vera gestured to Carda to let her do the talking. With ease Vera got them into the entrance hall. In the role of a location agent, Vera thanked her for her kindness in opening the door for them. She engaged Carda in a needless explanation of the advantages of the building while she waited for the woman to go on her way. They needed to avoid the routine cameras in the lifts and corridors. Once the woman had disappeared into the lift, Carda led Vera to the central courtyard from where he figured out the back door to the flat. The emergency stairs took them to the sixth floor. As they had imagined, the doors reinforced with access cards proved impenetrable without alerting the security systems. There were no windows but panels of solid glass. They reached Daniel Lo's door. Breaking the glass was not an option. Vera pressed the door lightly with a finger as if she knew it would be open. Neither of them expected it to give in easily. The curtain swayed on the other side of the glass as they entered without hesitation. Avoiding ABDs was a reflex action for both of them. Carda used the curtain to prevent the door from closing. Without an access card they would not be able to get out.

'Daniel.' Carda called out once and waited. 'He's not here.'

'Nobody leaves an access door open if they're not at home.'

'Maybe it was accidental.'

'It doesn't explain why he left by the back door.'

Carda and Vera noted things scattered all over the floor.

'Looks like he left in a hurry.'

'It does indeed.' Vera looked at the stuff on the floor by the table next to the door. In the bedroom, the screen in front of the bed was switched on. Bedclothes on the floor and a few clothes in the middle of them. Vera could not take a step without memories of that terrible night flooding back. She gazed at the clothes.

'We must look for the electronic logs.' Carda handed her a pair of gloves. 'Put these on.'

Again, Vera was not surprised by Carda's behaviour. He came prepared. Had he known what he would find in the flat? He was behaving like an expert investigator or like someone who knew what to look for. As usual, he did not reveal any more than was strictly necessary. Vera tried not to stray too far. It was essential that she be present if Carda found anything. She veered between complicity and mistrust. As they searched, they tried to leave things where they had found them.

'There's nothing.' Carda stood up in the middle of the room and looked around him. He looked impatiently at the time. More than five minutes in breach of security was an eternity.

'The food in the fridge has gone off. He's been missing for weeks.' Vera closed the fridge door.

While Carda looked in the fridge, Vera went to the back door. She could clearly see fingerprints on the edge of the glass. Behind the curtain, more prints which merged with someone else's. Two or three hands, perhaps. She imagined them struggling with each other. Trying to get in or out or both. She bent down and traced the fingerprints along the glass. It was when she was crouching down that she saw the membrane hooked onto two brackets on the underside of the table. Vera turned around to check that Carda was still poking around in the fridge. With her head against the edge of the table she stretched her arm as far as she could to reach it almost at the other end by the wall. Leaning on one hand she gently unhooked the rolled-up membrane. She was about to put it quickly into her jacket pocket…

'Well done,' Carda put out his hand. He was standing by the table watching her movements. Vera got up and put the membrane into his open hand. They eyed each other with uncertainty attempting to explore each other´s depths.

She would not let Carda take the membrane away with him nor did she expect him to let her have it. They both knew they would have to carry on together until they achieved clarity. Once back in her flat it took Vera a few minutes to decipher Daniel's password. Carda took charge of the membrane regardless of Vera´s unspoken wish. His excuse: that Vera should investigate Daniel's avatars and confirm or discard his link with *Cf* as a player.

They sat side by side, each with a membrane in front of them so as not to lose sight of the other's movements. It was late and they were tired. How long would Carda last without dropping exhausted onto the desk? Vera would not endure it much longer either. Her eyes were red after days of long hours of play.

'Dead? Another suicide? I don't think so,' Carda surmised.

'Whatever it is, it sounds irregular.' Vera figured Carda knew more than he was letting on. Each minute in silence in front of the membrane increased her sense of unease. Every time she could, Vera leant back to try to see the content of the screen in front of Carda.

'Look.' As if guessing her intentions, Carda spun the membrane on its axis with his finger. 'It can't be suicide. It's not on police records. It must be voluntary disappearance.'

'I don't understand. Do you think he was involved in the construction of *Cf*? In that case...'

'Not only would a bonus not be in order, but there aren't any irregular deposits in his account either. If he received this supposed bonus, either it was not money or it was under the counter.'

Vera stared at him.

'We should still make sure.' Though Vera was being more cautious with her assumptions, they appeared to understand each other perfectly within their differences.

It was dawn by the time Vera finished checking all the information in the thousands of PEF pages. Carda could barely hide the fact that he was nodding off. He sat up in his chair, startled by the voice next to him.

'I've finished checking all the records. He didn't play *VWCf* with any of his avatars. The chain of suicides linked to the game has been broken.'

'I knew it. So I hope he's written the code. If not, we have nothing.' Carda shook his head and forced his eyes open, squinting several times. 'I can't do any more. The letters are swimming before me.'

'We should rest.' For Vera it was a relief that Carda should admit to being tired.

'Zillo arrives tomorrow afternoon.'

'We won't get anywhere this way. We have several hours to carry on in his office tomorrow morning.'

Vera was not the only one to hide her mistrust. Carda was constantly analysing her attitudes. He would have to find out soon what Vera kept in the bedroom, which she not only considered private, but would not occupy that night. He was sure that sharing the living room with him would not have been her first choice. Carda would have to wait for an opportunity to open that door.

Vera increased the temperature in the living room and gestured towards the couch where Carda could lie down. On the other side of the room by the door to the bedroom Vera put an air mattress on the floor and pressed the button with her foot. The mattress shook as if coming to life and was ready in seconds. Vera lay down with her back to Carda. She switched off the lights with a voice command. The uncomfortable silence lasted longer than either of them wished. In spite of their exhaustion their eyes were open wider in the dark than they could bear.

She was not sure if Carda's deep breathing on the other side of the living room was threatening or protective. Had she underestimated him? Was it pure chance that she had not come home alone that night? They had not spent a minute apart. Even though she had not been forced, Vera felt tied to his presence. On his side of the room, Carda's breathing did not signal rest. Alert, he was waiting for Vera to fall asleep so that he could sneak into the bedroom. Getting to sleep would be so easy if they stopped struggling. If they caved in and began to trust one another.

The lights went on in the living room. Vera surfaced from a deep sleep. The daily music announcing the morning started up. It had been a long while since she had rested so serenely. On opening her eyes she almost forgot that Carda had slept at her flat. Or maybe not. She kept still with her eyes fixed on the ceiling. After those first seconds in which the mind adjusts to recall earlier events which lead to present consequences she sat on the mattress and looked warily towards the couch. The first thing was to check that Carda was still there. It was what she had dreaded. The couch was empty. Vera jumped up, ran to the bedroom and opened the door. It was all just as it had been. Except that Carda was not in the flat. Neither was Daniel's membrane.

She chewed her tooth tablet and reflected as she cycled to Vatican Inc. Her intuition had almost disappeared. She did not know what to think. She could only review the absurdity of her actions. All she had to do was turn back, take from her flat the few things she would need to survive. Just leave, as she had wanted to do year after year. There was nothing left to reflect on or consider now. On the contrary, if she carried on she would be increasingly entangled in something unimaginably obscure. She risked a punishment which could compromise her freedom for ever. For ever. The decision had never been clearer. Free will was an aspect of her personality she had barely cultivated. Now it pushed her like an unstoppable current.

Vera went into the building as if giving herself up for sacrifice. When she opened the door to Zillo's office, there was Carda with Daniel's membrane. Even if he offered her an explanation, Carda had broken the trust Vera had bestowed on him when she allowed herself to fall asleep. That was enough. Even worse, Vera did not know that he had gone into her bedroom before leaving the flat. He had left her asleep with no possibility of making any decisions. Carda's intentions were more of an unknown entity than ever. Vera approached slowly, expecting a reaction.

'The brain has around one hundred million neurons. Each neuron is a collection of atoms. Like the components of a computer.' Carda was talking obsessively. Nothing mattered more than the information he had begun to churn out in a fit of revelation. 'Brain waves have different frequencies. In the physical world, thought occurs at twenty cycles per second, four when asleep. If it's done at ten cycles per second, thought is balanced.' Carda offered Vera Daniel's membrane. Vera remained standing a short distance away.

'The method is explained in this document. The right-hand side of the brain governs intuition, imagination. It's the dormant side. It is tyrannised by the left-hand side which deals with the physical world, reason, logic and efficiency. Only rarely does the brain operate at intermediate frequencies, except when passing from wakefulness to sleep or vice versa. However, it's the intermediate frequencies that provide the conscious use of the brain's right hemisphere, our spiritual connection. For this the ideal frequency is ten cycles per second, known as the "alpha level".'

Carda, immersed in his customary intensity, in spite of his stubble and haggard look, was devoted more than ever to the task in order to isolate himself from other thoughts. He was not going to mention it, but the traces in the bedroom had been poignant. When Carda had entered that room chaos had become ordered in unmistakable signs. What Vera could recall as hurt, Carda felt in his imagination. The deep-seated realisation of what he had never had. That room revealed it in a single, incorruptible flash. The love that survived in the chaos. There Carda was an intruder. On leaving he had shut the door with a delicacy of which he had never been capable before.

The files in Daniel's membrane gave him back his presence of mind. Vera went up to Carda. The distance again seemed insurmountable.

'*Vatican World Cf* interferes with the alpha state, the state of connection to intuition, spiritual wisdom, proximity to…' Carda avoided naming it if he could. 'In scientific terms, it activates the right hemisphere of the brain to connect with the morphogenetic field. It's the same thing as harmonising intelligence with a higher understanding, in spiritual terms. Religious people call it God. Others, a higher intelligence.'

'So why does it provoke the opposite, the destruction of beings?'

Carda raised his hand without looking up. Although he did not have the answer he continued reciting the information to avoid letting that tenuous but emphatic moment of understanding escape.

'According to this paper, the left brain is characterised by separation, difference, polarity, constant duality. The right brain does not see differences, but equality. On balancing the perception of differences, we are in harmony with the superior intelligence. The human brain has psychotronic energy which can be programmed. I think there can be only one conclusion to this. The game manipulates the right-hand side of the user's brain.'

PART VIII

Zillo entered through the side door straight into Martino's office. He left his briefcase on the table. Ten screens reproduced in miniature the fifty screens in the security room next door.

'They've been there all morning.' Martino touched the screen so that Zillo could listen to the conversations from an hour earlier. Zillo scrolled through using the surface of the screen, choosing the moments. Just a few seconds of conversation were enough for him to know what they were talking about.

'So we have nothing from yesterday.'

'I enabled the cameras in your office when you asked me to this morning.'

From Martino's office Zillo watched the images with a blend of incredulity and bewilderment. Martino stood waiting looking blankly at the stone inner courtyard. He didn't like to draw any conclusions. He left that to his boss. He felt much more comfortable just following orders. Zillo removed the card. The live images being activated made him react. Yes, it was Carda and Vera in his own office.

'...something which the user can't fight against.'

'We must contact the World Government right away.'

'We can't do it from here. Don't go away. I have an idea.' Carda left Zillo's office.

'It's essential to neutralise him. I'll take care of Vera. I need her.' Zillo had recovered. Martino left his office impassive.

Zillo pressed Individual Tracking and sat in front of the two screens. The ones which in a few minutes would put an end to years of collaborative work. The lines on Zillo's face seemed suddenly to deepen while he followed Carda's footsteps down the corridor on the screen.

'I could have asked you to write the code for the entire *Cf*.

I didn't want you to pay such a high price. I tried to avoid it. Daniel was dispensable. Not you. Now you leave me with no choice. I saved your life and this is how you repay me. I can't help you.' Zillo laid the palm of his hand on the cold surface in front of him. He lifted the headset from the desk.

'He's coming here. Let him in first.'

Carda knocked on the door.

'Come in.' Zillo, his back to the door, continued staring fixedly at the screens. Vera in his office was reading the documents which should not have fallen into her hands.

Carda opened the door and saw Zillo in silhouette sitting with his back to him in the swivel chair.

'Martino?'

With his feet firmly on the ground Father Zillo spun the chair around. The usual smile, as if he had been expecting him. Carda was stunned by the image before he blacked out and fell to the ground at Martino's feet. The Head of Security pushed Carda's limp body aside. Father Zillo avoided looking at the ground. It was an absurd scene, witnessing his golden boy felled like a criminal.

'You know what you have to do.' Zillo left the office to find Vera.

Vera was processing the information Carda had revealed to her. While she read the document on Daniel's membrane she asked herself who Carda was and why he was bent on the same search as her own. He was a reserved man. He had been unpleasant and competitive. Maybe Vera's perception did not reflect what he had expressed. It had been her interpretation. She had let herself be swayed by circumstance. Perhaps her perception had been as wrong with so many other things. Once again reality was not what her senses suggested. The truth slithered away to show another truth which had been hidden. She wondered if that truth would slip away again to reveal that it wasn't real either.

Zillo entered his office with his usual calm air. Vera was pleased to see him. His was the only face she recognised from the past. Like Benedita, Father Zillo had always been there. To support her, to give her an opportunity. The congregation had many reasons to be grateful to him.

'Father, thank goodness you're here. Have you seen Carda?'

'Yes, he's with Martino.'

'Has he explained it to you? There's a problem in *Cf*.'

'He only said you were going to explain something to me.'

'First I need to ask you something.'

'Tell me, Vera.'

'Is Daniel Lo the confidential *Cf* programmer?'

'As you've said. It's a confidential security matter.'

'I know, Father. But I have here his membrane. It doesn't specifically mention *Cf*. But we believe he has interfered with the code. We found a document suggesting as much.'

'Have you spoken to Daniel?'

'No, Father.'

'You've appropriated his membrane.'

'I know it's not right. It was necessary.'

'What are you suggesting, Vera?'

'We believe there is a subliminal device in *Cf* which is responsible for the suicide of thousands of people who play the game regularly.'

'There's no need to start panicking. Whatever it is that's not working will be corrected. An attack by the media would destroy *Vatican World*. It would do irreparable harm.'

'We must find Daniel Lo.'

'You're the best, Vera. There's no need to involve anyone else. I shouldn't say something that gives me away,' Zillo tried a smile. 'but obviously the years have taken their toll on him. I thought Daniel was on good form. He has been out of the industry for too long. You could rewrite the code in due time and replace it.'

'That could take weeks. We can't wait. The population is killing itself. We must alert the Department of National Security so that they can alert the World Government. We should recall the product.'

Sitting in front of Daniel's membrane, Zillo read the document which had inspired Vera and Carda to make up this extraordinary story.

'Forgive me for mentioning the event. Is it possible that your partner's unexpected demise has nourished this fantasy? Is this the only proof you have of something that doesn't work?'

'Father, it's something that interferes with users' spirit.'

'What a thing to say!'

'I know it sounds ludicrous. We have no conclusive proof. That's why we need to warn the population through the World Government.'

Father Zillo turned to Vera with an unrecognisable look. Vera's proposal was trivial compared to his all-encompassing vision. The universal scope he had to bear in mind when making decisions.

'Who do you think you are to alert the World Government? You're being arrogant. Arrogance is not only the worst sin, but the origin of all the others. Do you think yourself somehow above humanity? Would you deny it a basic need? I'm talking about living in harmony. We have reached this state of grace after millennia of struggles and violence. Do you want to destroy that grace we have conquered? Child, don't you realise you're challenging God?'

'People all over the world are taking their own lives.'

'It's an error that will be put right. How do you know that the World Government is not aware of it?'

'People should know about it. They should stop playing the game until the error has been corrected.'

'People want to live in peace. That's why they leave the responsibility of managing the world to us and the World Government. It's a better world. You were lucky to have been born in it. I knew the previous one. The one you didn't know had millions paying for loans with no way out. That was how the world was controlled back then. Do you know how many people were born and died in poverty?'

There was a sacred silence which lasted for the time Zillo bowed his head as if in contrition. Vera was left unable to reply given the dimension of Father Zillo's arguments. The priest recovered his breath and looked her in the eye again.

'If they stop playing the game, they won't take it up again.'

'Is this the only option?'

'No. This is the third option. The world was distanced from God in any case. I've struggled to make it possible. I will take charge of rectifying the error with no need to return to times of panic. You can help me.' Zillo's smile bewildered her.

'Don't ask me to help you avoid people becoming aware of this.'

'Aware? That's a nice word. Their manipulation is absolutely necessary. You'll have seen a dog without the control of the leader of the pack – It doesn't know what to do – it becomes neurotic or aggressive. We have managed to put an end to the good of the privileged few. We have preserved a world at peace. Basic needs are covered. We must continue to protect this world. The next step is to end the ideal of a freedom that is linked to economic priorities. Commercial exchange at the expense of human exchange. Complacency and superficiality at the expense of spiritual greatness and elevation. That's my mission. The only way is to preserve a creed which is internalised in the majority. Religion should thrive. Politicians will finally come to understand. What societies need in order to survive is cohesion.'

'Manipulating the mind. Your practices, Father, are no different from those of the World Government.'

'For their own good. It's nothing new. Haven't you yourself lived the consequences of the inability to live together, egocentrism, evil? Man is a mental patient, dangerous to society and himself. It's necessary to protect humanity from its own madness. Have you read Céline? The human condition can't change because it is made of stinking mud.'

'Why should those in control be any different?'

'Justice doesn't exist in the way you imagine it. Pacts of interest will always exist. Some benefit at one time, and others, other times. Meanwhile, keeping the population carefree and happy is an enormous task. Those of us who understand the world carry the burden of knowing that it's a delicate balance. Before the cataclysm the economy was based on war. Of course such a system was going to collapse one day. Don't you think a source of income based on games is preferable?'

'Have you ever stepped back, as if outside your own body? To look around you, the people in this room, the announcements on the big screen, the speeches, the launches. Games are nothing other than a way of control. They are not necessary for life.'

'Games are the food on the table. Can't you see? Now we *can* live. Technology has protected everyone. Human ingenuity has managed to save the world.'

'From what?'

'You can't have it all. There will always have to be a losing side. The virtual world has the ability to take us to a new world.'

'It locks us up in a false one.'

'You're so ungrateful. After the cataclysm, humanity has managed to flourish so that individuals can attain equality. Now they can also aspire to more. I'm happy to have found a way. We only need to perfect it.'

'Father, what is there in *Cf*?'

Vera had no fear. What nurtured her gave her the composure with which she joined Father Zillo at the huge panelled window overlooking the hundreds of employees sitting passively at their screens.

'Are you going to help me?'

'Look at them. They're dead. Alienated from a life they don't understand.'

'What life would that be, Vera? Do you mean nature, the cosmos? Nature has turned her back on us. The cosmos has always been alien and distant. What we have is this.'

Zillo swept his arm over the extensive processing room at his feet.

'You believe in God. Like everyone, you prefer to protect yourself from mystery.'

'Just like Adam and Eve in Paradise, you and Carda have betrayed me. It's a shame you don't want to help thousands of people. They will continue to kill themselves until the problem is solved.' Zillo took out of his pocket a gun so small it looked like a toy. 'Armchair philosophy has been relegated to self-help books from before the cataclysm. This is reality. Those books have been superseded by games. You said it. It's not right but it's necessary.'

Zillo raised the gun and pointed it at her. Vera looked at him, suspended in incredulity. The absurdity of the gun in the priest's hand paralysed her. The man who had opened the doors for her and had admired her. Now he was ready to take it all away from her. What was the overriding objective? The one that made it possible for a man to decide to suppress a life? Vera reverted almost unwittingly to a primitive state. One by one her limbs numbed until she felt only her spirit spreading around the room. She barely smiled on perceiving Father Zillo's naivety with the minuscule gun in his hand. The vastness of the universe ahead of his act of supreme obtuseness. The magnitude of his purpose was dissolved in the wave of energy rising from Vera's body as if once more her head opened to the cosmos to understand nothing. To be immaterial with the immensity of a truth as certain as it was unknown. Like in a photo, Zillo's image was recorded once more among hundreds of billions of futile, useless, empty scenes. Scenes piled up over centuries of history. Evolution with no evolution. Meaningless. The image of Zillo holding a gun could summarise them and at the same time encompass them all, the same ones. It was one. Vera knew it and there she remained, feeling nothing but the moment of departure to be as one with her moon.

PART IX

The blast from the shot filled the room to echo in the air above the hundreds of operators sitting in silence. Its fallout, millions of shards of glass. A white rain on top of the heads, now bowed, of those perplexed by the glass drops. Until from the gaping hole in the vast window upstairs the black shape began to fall. Their astonishment was cut short by the dull thud as Father Zillo's body hit the ground.

Roch emerged from behind the screen with the gun still in his hand. The resounding crash of the glass restored Vera's bodily sensations. Roch was still pointing the gun, his arm stretched out. As if his own action had petrified him. Turning her body slightly, Vera just had time to assimilate events on the other side of the glass. The door opened suddenly and Carda fell into the room. Martino, who had pushed Carda's body using it to enter, closed the door, dropping the handkerchief with which he had covered a deep gash on his forehead. At that point it became clear to Vera who Carda was. It was good news on the one hand, twice as bad on the other, when she saw the guns both Roch and Martino were pointing at her. At the same time as Carda's heavy breathing against the floor suggested he was injured.

'Roch, where's Zillo?' The blood from his forehead did not allow Martino to see the open space left by the shattered glass panel. 'Help me with these. Come on, get moving!'

Roch seemed to have lost control of his muscles. In a catatonic state he barely turned his head to look at Martino who had picked up the handkerchief and was wiping off the blood clouding his vision.

'Didn't you hear me? Where's Zillo?'

For the first time Martino paid attention to the scene. It was very straightforward. Everything was clearly set out. So clear that he could not see what was evident when he entered and became a part of it. The only thing Martino managed to see was so extraordinary that he became thoroughly confused. He saw the open space where the glass panel should have been, its absence confirmed by the voices he could hear rising from the processing room. If Roch held a gun pointed at Vera and she was still standing next to the empty space of the glass, where was Zillo? The simplicity of the scene made no sense to Martino. It became even more senseless when, on turning his head towards Roch, he felt the impact on his chest. Or seconds later when, even if he did not feel the second impact, another bullet perforated his temple. Neither of the bullets that were shot at him made sense to Vera. Martino fell dead on top of Carda. Without analysing the scene Vera ran to help him to free himself of the unbearable weight of the towering security guard. Neither of them saw Roch turn the gun into his own mouth. To use the last bullet and end his own life too.

Vera struggled to drag Martino to one side. The sound of the fourth bullet had shocked her. She had not expected it. She did not need to look at Roch to know that he had been its target. Given the sequence of events, she was glad Carda was not holding a gun too. Guns had been in unexpected hands, except in Martino's case. Shots had also been fired at those least expecting them. Other questions arose: had Roch seen the priest pointing his gun at her and had he shot Zillo to protect her. If he had had no choice but to shoot Martino why had he turned the gun on himself? What was the explanation for all this? It was like one of the games which she had so categorically refused to play.

Carda stood up with Vera's help. The burning sensation at the back of his neck matched the dizziness from which he had not yet recovered.

'Carda, are you all right?'

'My name is Felix.' He touched her hand with the same lightness with which Vera breathed her surprise.

'What happened?'

'When I went into his office Martino knocked me out… He cut his forehead but he had a gun.' Vera did not ask for explanations as Carda's confused summary did nothing to clarify what had happened.

Disorientated, Carda could not explain the chain of events to Vera. On entering the office, Martino had hit him on the back of the head. Carda had lost consciousness for a few minutes. When he came to, he found he was half inside a crate. Martino was holding him, his arms wrapped around his chest. It only took a fraction of the clarity he was regaining to understand that Martino was about to despatch him to the darkest of fates. A healthy impulse for survival had allowed Carda the strength he needed to give an unsuspecting Martino a shove. Despite slipping and banging his forehead on the metal edge of the console, Martino had managed to regain control of the situation. At least it had alerted him to what the monitors were showing. Although for Vera it was a mystery that Carda should know what had happened in Zillo's office.

'I think it was when Roch shot Zillo… We didn't see it. We only saw that Roch was pointing a gun at where you were standing. On another monitor the processing room operators could be seen standing in a circle. It was lucky that Martino didn't see Zillo in the middle of it. He saw just enough to bring me here.'

'There are no cameras here.' The knock on the head had confused him but Vera did not realise that Carda's explanation was totally coherent.

'Yes there are, they're hidden. I imagine they connect them when Zillo says so. Said so. I've just seen the images in Martino's office.'

'So, had you seen that Zillo had fallen?'

'No. I imagined it. I knew that bullet was for Zillo. It was a relief to see you still standing.'

Vera could only figure out what was most obvious. Carda was being laconic again. This time she thought it understandable. Carda peered cautiously through the window. A group of police officers and building security staff were dispersing the operators. They had placed Zillo's body on two of the tables. The light from the terminals on one side of the body made his blood-soaked face glisten red.

'We have little time. It won't be long before the police come here.' Carda removed the access card from Zillo's screen.

'I don't understand.'

'We have to get into Daniel's code and modify whatever it is he's done in *Cf*. We'll at least have time to neutralise the code before the IPSs are triggered.'

'Without access? We must talk to the police to...'

'I'll explain later.' Felix gripped her by the shoulders, agitated. 'We must go to your office. *Now*.'

Felix grabbed her hand. Vera's intuition assured her there was no reason to doubt him. They went out into the corridor.

'We mustn't run but we need to hurry.' Felix let go of her hand.

They walked past the cameras with restrained haste. They reached the side corridor and, once the access door shut behind them, ran downstairs to avoid the police who were coming up in the lifts. Carda knew he could not rely on the entire security force of the building to have made their way to the processing room. They would gain time if nobody could see where they were. Vera went into her office. Felix followed her and without delay picked up the little table at the entrance. He put it under one of the cameras. He climbed onto it and pointed the lens to the ceiling. He jumped off the table and with equal urgency did the same with the other camera. Now it would just be a question of luck. He was confident he had moved sufficiently fast. If nobody came into the office in the next few minutes, they would have a bit more time; security and the police would have their hands full with what they would find in Zillo's office. When he jumped for the second time Felix again felt the impact on the nape of his neck. As he staggered, Vera went to him to offer her arm and she held him up. There was an intense warmth in Carda's tight clasp. Vera allowed herself to be embraced. Those brief seconds restored in Felix a feeling of trust long forgotten.

'It was him. Thanks for giving me an excuse.' He was embarrassed by his own choked voice.

'Who?' Vera no longer hid her confusion at the chain of events.

'I'm sorry.' Carda drew away from the consolation he took from Vera's warm body. The silence between them had changed. He no longer felt it served to impose himself. Felix sat in the armchair at the back of the room. Vera opened the screen avoiding his eyes, watching him in its reflection.

The time had come. The explanations Carda had kept to himself were compellingly linked to recent events. For all he knew, they might both end up under arrest. If revealing the truth might bring them punishment.

'I know what you think about the World Government. The World Church is not much better. Past powers legitimised actions using religions. Since their merging, they no longer interfere with the government, nor the government with them. After the cataclysm they were left to their own devices.' Vera continued in silence with the procedures on the screen, not missing a word. 'The general synod of bishops was the first to seek solutions to the Catholic Church's loss of power. The main criterion was economic. Without any money, the Church had no way of continuing or progressing, just like any political party. They ended up not caring that church goers would ignore moral guidance. With the church business they finally admitted their intention to regain their power. They agreed to provide the basis for peaceful living. Compliance with canons took second place. The synod found only one way out. To adhere to the main principle of the modern world: lack of satisfaction in the individual. Consumerism its opium. Forgetting about death. The memory of the cataclysm was too recent.'

To Vera his image on the screen had never seemed so clear. She wondered how somebody could be so different from the way others saw them. Carda's image was refreshed. It was not all appearances like the previous one. Then it became real as he began to speak.

'The decline of the Church gathered speed as clergymen were caught *in flagrante*. Money from public funds spent in whorehouses. The Church paid billions in damages for the sexual abuse of children for decades. They covered it up but it leaked out. I'm sure that Benedita never spoke to you about it. Thousands of cases on file. They could have prevented other victims from suffering the same fate. Complaints that were never recorded. The Vatican would tell its bishops to cover up cases of sexual abuse or they risked excommunication. The Church consented to a culture of deceit and concealment. I've been here for years. For years I was trained for this job. For years I was scared of doing anything.'

'Why you?'

'I was one of those children. The idea of revenge grew so much that it paralysed me. When I was twenty Zillo swapped me for somebody younger. Roch is the fourth. He had already reached the age of twenty-four. I wondered why he kept him for so long. Now I see why. Roch also undertook other tasks. Trained by Martino, probably. There were clothes at the bottom of the crate he pushed me into. I have no doubt that they were Daniel's. When I read the document on Daniel's membrane, it all fell into place.'

'Why would he want to get rid of Daniel?'

'Haven't you seen enough to know?' It did not take Carda long to show he had not lost his harshness.

No. It was not easy for Vera to take in the existence of a small universe of which she had no experience and to which Carda had been exposed. Where behaviours, although simple, were crudely entangled. Once again Vera experienced, through Carda, what it meant to distrust intentions. The actions and consequences of power. Aspects of living without enlightenment. One lot against another. One lot in favour of another. One lot above another. The mind acting stubbornly. Simply on the grounds of purpose. She did not want to let on that what Carda had revealed had moved her deeply. She sensed he did not want her pity.

Felix would never again mention the matter. Those few words said it all. Explanations were but minor details. The stories of so many fallen by the wayside were barely linked to the present of a few. However tough their experiences, these had ceased to be a topic of conversation. The past was mentioned in terms of world history. Events without their interpretation. The World Government was bent on ensuring the population looked to the future. For this it promoted the present through systems which easily moulded it. Personal lives did not persist in memory. Nobody wanted to remember or be reminded. As if each person were nothing but a present being. With no background or origin outside of today.

If Felix would have to tell his personal story, he would have been able to narrate it around three events. With the cataclysm, everything else had seemed insignificant. Even if it wasn't. Even if those three events had affected him to the extent that he became Carda. In time Carda had had to leave Felix aside as self-protection against vulnerability. What Vera did not imagine was that Carda's detachment had not arisen as a result of the abuse by Zillo. Nor of the death of his parents in the cataclysm.

As a child his parents had been mostly absent. Even though their weeks spent at home were infrequent, the company of the governess or the maid was not sufficient either. He did not blame anyone for their busy lives. It was what he knew. Felix clung to children's technology. In his efforts to overcome extended periods in the great empty spaces at home. Finding company was a surprise. The nearest mansion was a third of a mile away on the other side of the fence separating the two properties. At the far end of the gardens surrounding his gigantic prison, he was riding his bicycle one afternoon when he was drawn to a voice coming from the other side of the fence. Through the almost perfect wall of intertwined greenery he spied on his neighbour as she played with her cat. A little girl, a child just like him left alone amid the abundance of money. They did not take long to cross the barrier, nor did it prevent them from playing even on the first few afternoons. They grew familiar with each other, the hedge in between. They sought each other out in the little gaps they discovered in the long tall hedge, where the cat would appear held by the girl to make Felix laugh. By the end of a few days the decision had been made. Felix slipped into the shed to take some pruning shears and open a way through. Once they could traverse the hedge as if by magic, they would both forget the coldness that surrounded them. They soon ceased caring. Felix would come on his bicycle every afternoon to take his neighbour away during the hours between lunch and supper. Neither of them had ever had as much fun as on their adventures entering the house unseen. The freedom they felt on hiding without anybody missing her. Complicity opened up a new world.

They were as only children can be. A few days after their parents died in the cataclysm, they were in the attic where they spent hours exchanging secrets. Nothing would shake them when they were together, not even finding the bodies of the maid and the governess in the corridors of the mansion as if death had discovered them running from one end to the other. They had run together too, to the attic. To save themselves in the only place where everything was familiar to them. With childish intuition they had not waited for their parents, who would not come back.

They had loaded bags and rucksacks with everything they thought they would need from the pantry and kitchen. They looked at each other, eyes wide open, when they realised that they were free to eat whatever they wanted, whenever they wanted. There were enough provisions to last for a long while. They would live in the attic. There Felix and the little girl, orphaned, protected themselves from the world. They had created a safe space where they surrounded themselves with things that were constant. For her, the blanket which would leave yellow fluff everywhere, storybooks, socks with leather soles, her rabbit-eared cap. For him, the little tent, the coloured torch, the e-pad loaded with games. The things that made them forget. The cat made complete their desire not to let that feeling of well-being escape in the middle of the chaos they sensed would ensue. They watched the television images almost like a forbidden film. The outside was veiled by closed curtains which they had never opened again. Although it might have seemed so at first, they were not there on holiday. As the girl felt the weight of reality, Felix promised her that they would not let in the horror which was unfolding on the cataclysmic streets. Weeks went by in the inner normality of their adventure. They rarely dared go downstairs to fetch something from the house which for them had become a huge warehouse. Felix would do all he could to preserve that normality. Everything except what he could not possibly prevent. Weeks later, when the poison also reached the girl, Felix had time to tell her he loved her. Even at the tender age of ten. From then on everything had become confused and uncertain. He could not remember how he had ended up at the academy. The events had stunned him into silence. Zillo sensed that coolness from the beginning. On the outside it gave Felix a set face and on the inside an unnoticed fragility. It was to this that Zillo had appealed so that Felix would devote himself to him.

Felix inserted Zillo's card into Vera's screen and she let him have her seat. He followed the security stages automatically as though fearing a reaction to what he had said. He carried on working at the screen while he sensed Vera's presence behind him like a warm feeling.

'When Zillo called me to put me in charge of the project, he took control of the code out of my hands. He had never before hidden anything from me. I thought something had changed. In spite of the new security rules, it was only a suspicion. Your behaviour made me distrust him even more. When I understood what you were trying to find out, it confirmed that my demented thoughts had a sound basis. Now I'm certain that something in *Cf* is activated on the right-hand side of the brain.'

'For what purpose?'

'Zillo's favourite phrase, "to save the planet and heal ourselves". In all these years… if I know Zillo's aspirations… To restore the Church's worldwide power.'

'You mean to force people into believing in God again? It doesn't explain the suicides.'

'It's possible that by programming the right brain in daily contact with the left brain it would lay bare the contradiction between them. I've read a few books on existential angst in Zillo's library. They suggest we have let the intuitive side die. Eighty percent of suicides are among the male population. In spite of the cataclysm, reason continues to override everything. The lack of contact with the right side of the brain allows differences in the left-hand side to take over people's personal lives and govern actions. With more brains focusing in this way, the effect would become cumulative and give rise to a collective conscience. The cybernetic effect would accelerate the change exponentially.'

'We must get into the code.' Vera finally accepted the urgency. As if so many scattered, unconnected phrases arranged themselves together to make up an unquestionably clear text. 'If the intention is not to provoke suicide but to induce control, it could be an error in the code.'

'An error or something worse.'

Vera and Carda knew that even if they used Zillo's card to access Daniel's code, intrusion prevention systems would log the anomaly. To access an operative code they had to gain authorisation. Only in this way would the IPSs be switched off before accessing it. They had no other choice but to enter without access. Even if IPSs were triggered the crisis in the building gave them more leeway to operate in the electronic systems.

'Impossible.' Carda banged his fist on the table. 'Daniel used a new language. Without knowing it it's impossible to decode.'

'The problem with parameters has to be at the top level. I've played hundreds of times. I reached the penultimate level. I haven't managed to get to the fifth. I've created dozens of games engines. Playing them is not my thing.'

'We're back to square one.'

'No. I'm going to enter the game. Just like all the others.'

'We don't know exactly what it is. It could be dangerous.'

'Galo reached the last level. So did the others. I must get into Galo's account.'

'We don't have much time. Do you have the password?'

'There aren't many possibilities. It won't take me more than a few minutes to decipher it.' Vera did not wait for Felix's answer. She put her hand on his shoulder. It was her turn at the screen. She sat down while Felix observed her closely. In less than ten seconds Vera had the password.

'I'm going in with Lark. Straight to level five.'

'Are you sure?' Felix handed her the control glove and the special sensor.

Vera connected the access key and the projection card. Movement sensors received the first signal. She looked to her right, towards the only window in the room.

'Felix, please, open the window.'

The darkness outside could be sensed from the office flooded with light. The moon was not there.

'Turn the light off.'

The sensors already recognised every movement. Facial or bodily. Her mood and emotions would be simultaneously logged, informing the game every step of the way. The choice of events would then be set up at each stage according to frame of mind and points scored. She adjusted the glove. Not only would it allow her to run at high speed. It would also transmit tactile information.

'rewotym.' Vera contained herself as she pronounced the name. Galo had used that password countless times in her absence. The avatar which had led him to his death. On pressing Start the image emerged from the screen and covered the whole room in 3D. Vera was already inside the game. She was entering the alternative life Galo had created in his final months. The only one to which he had not given her access. Lark was a passionate character. Was it the real Galo expressing himself freely in a world where everything was possible? Total and at the same time inexistent risk. Lark had a physical strength equal to the passion of his spirit. Vera settled into that body to live out Galo's hopes. To make it as far as Lark had.

PART X

The code had had a sudden effect like a final blow to the human psyche.

Vera had reached the fourth level. She had managed to get inside the game and feel the force of something she could not define. Now she knew it was there. A destructive interference, erroneous messages. Vera was there to understand it all.

Although Lark knew very well where to go, it was now no longer Galo who controlled him. Vera faced frighteningly unfamiliar territory. She kept telling herself that she must breathe steadily. The simplest of tasks now became difficult for Vera. She had to return to the basic principles she had known from birth when entering a realm where the slightest error could lead to her downfall.

She was taken by surprise. On entering the fifth level, Lark took flight into his favourite scenario. The sheer terrain of the Dolomites. He would be facing the creatures and events which protected the chest containing the Holy Book. Vera was unfamiliar with Lark's attributes. Finding out what they were as she went along was a dangerous process. Not only did she have to fine-tune his movements, speed and distances in flight. The imposing scenery was new to her and inhospitable. The game was about to start. She had seconds to get ready. At any moment the challenges would appear. She had just begun when she became aware of the first obstacle. Lark's wings restricted the use of weapons and ammunition. Then something else became evident. In addition to being a neophyte at a new level, Vera's inexperience and lack of knowledge about the avatar would not only reduce her chances of reaching catharsis, it would also make it very difficult to survive. Vera knew she had to bring in Clarissa. If she incorporated her as an additional player she would be able to substitute

Galo's unexplored environment for the familiar context of the Vatican.

'Felix.' Vera could no longer see him but she needed him.

'Yes, Vera. I'm here.'

'I'm going to need the other glove. Quick. I'm going to bring in my own avatar.'

'You shouldn't go in with multiple players if you're the only user. If you're not an advanced player...'

'The glove!' She had neither the time nor any way of explaining to Felix. Lark and Clarissa had to play together. It was their only chance.

While Vera eluded the birds of prey swooping against Lark in his reconnaissance flight, Felix slipped onto her hand the control glove that would give Clarissa entry.

'Thanks.' Vera turned her head. She knew she was not alone.

Not only had Clarissa never reached the fifth level. She did not know Lark nor the steep landscape he inhabited. The first contact with Lark would be vital. Any decision crucial for both of them. Vera regained confidence on seeing Clarissa at the summit of Mount Pelmo. There she was ready to join Lark in the task of overcoming any obstacle and reaching catharsis. On the other side of the mountain, Lark had outwitted the birds of prey and was preparing to seek out the cave in which the chest was kept. It was the perfect moment for them to meet. Once they had done so, Lark would fly with Clarissa to Vatican City.

The game had not stopped. It was only Vera's false impression, in her desire to materialise a dreamt up moment. Lark and Clarissa. A meeting. Seconds after bringing in her avatar she had not even seen the rocks rolling off the cliff and crashing at Clarissa's feet. The roar of the earthquake which split open the rock into deep crevasses alerted her too late. Clarissa went over the cliff towards the bottom of the canyon like a wingless bird. Vera felt in her own body the inertia propelling Clarissa towards certain death. She managed to hold on to her seat struggling against the feeling of wanting to let go until she felt the force behind the tug which clutched at her belly. Lark held Clarissa's hand to lift her up into a strong embrace and fly away.

The encounter had not only been flawless. It had taken her breath away. Once settled into the flight, Vera familiarised herself with the possibilities she had at her fingertips. To be successful she had to learn and adapt quickly. The association between Lark and Clarissa began to work as Vera had hoped. While Lark flew over the terrain, Clarissa used the weapons familiar to Vera. Her experience at level four turned out to be more valuable than she had thought. If she adapted to the fifth level from the beginning, her confidence would be boosted and she would stay away from any unexpected threat the game might throw at her.

Vera focused on getting them to the city intact. The blue of Lake Garda hardly compared to that of the Adriatic they would see to the east. If they kept a good altitude they would have a greater chance of collecting points using the capacity to fly, instead of having to battle against storms or fierce birds. The only danger they faced was air traffic. Clarissa alerted Lark to any movements from behind. Like children they enjoyed the aerodynamic excitement that Vera was fast learning to control. Passing over the Lombardy plains they joined the central spine of the Apennines. They flew over it at dangerous speed. The obstacles would become faster and heavier. These were no longer just tourist spacecraft, fighter or hypersonic airplanes. Space station waste, satellite debris or meteorites entering the atmosphere also conspired against them. To obliterate them on impact with no chance of survival. In Lark's arms Clarissa filled Vera with astonishing confidence. For a few minutes she forgot about the importance of her task. They dodged aircraft, destroyed projectiles, defended themselves against unexpected missiles. Vera surrendered to the pleasure of the game. With Clarissa and Lark transporting her far away from the pressing reality. Taking her to that which was set in a virtual world. Where she had sensed she might have once arrived with Galo.

Lark and Clarissa sealed their virtual commitment in flight. They established an essential link, confident they would reach the end together. They followed the Tiber like a fertile serpent to the gates of Rome. Vera felt a pull in the glove at the same time that Lark and Clarissa unexpectedly changed direction. It had not been Vera who had diverted the course to the east. Lark pointed in the distance. They had reached the place Clarissa had earlier whispered in his ear. She held his arm while they came closer to allow Vera to see. They flew over the area hoping that Vera would recognise it straightaway. Like all virtual locations, the game projected the original landscape, free from mechanised intrusions, the way not even Vera had known it. Though it looked different, without the white needles or the panels which surrounded it, Vera knew the place. Lark's Wood and its lake looked even more splendid from the air. If their purpose for taking Vera to this meaningful forest was for encouragement before embarking on the last stage of the game, her smile proved they had succeeded. Clarissa and Lark felt in their own bodies the intimacy Vera retained in her memory. When Lark moved closer to Clarissa to kiss her, Vera forced herself to come back to the pressing moment and regained control to take them back to Rome.

Once they completed the flight stage they had the highest score. Clarissa had been empowered. The fifth level was no longer forbidden to her.

Lark was in an environment he was not made for. In the Quo Vadis church Clarissa covered his wings with a black cape. He must not attract attention. She knew the guards' tricks and the city's traps. Above all, she knew the hidden corners, the agendas and itineraries of the place. Her knowledge was valuable but not sufficient. The fifth level had new elements. The gates to Vatican City would not open until they passed the ultimate trial. The greatest challenge of all.

They had now reached the final test. To acquire new power-ups, it was necessary to choose the surprise option. She had not imagined that the surprise would be the environment. The unforeseen setting which began to unfold disturbed Vera. It would not be an easy transition. Her sensory response was compromising her progress. She should not be fearful if she was determined to reach her goal. The 3D extension of the St Callistus catacombs made Felix rise from his seat. He did not know that setting. If the sector came from Daniel's work, perhaps Vera had reached the final stage. Vera shivered with the frozen presence underground. The burnt, crucified martyrs, the popes in their stone niches. Half a million lifeless bodies. The narrow passageway to the galleries where ghoulish figures had come to their final rest.

Flaming torches in hand, Clarissa and Lark set off overcoming the first obstacle. At the entrance at the end of the stairway the giant spider clung to its dense web. Her slow movements did not prevent her agile legs from being a pointed threat while a colony of bats tried to distract them and push them towards her sticky trap. It was an agility test. The limited space left no room for the slightest slip. Clarissa and Lark looked at each other and smiled. Up in the skies they had passed a much more difficult test of movement. Clarissa cast the net she had taken out of her boot, catching the colony of bats and hurling them against the spider's web. The feast on offer was far too tempting. The spider immediately diverted her attention. She now chewed insatiably on the bats' heads, the stricken animals flapping their wings in a vain attempt to escape. Each one left staked alongside the spider. After piercing the viscous interior of her head with a sword, Lark opened up a gap in the web to step through. The spider did not respond, while the wings of the bats still flapped, hanging from her mouth.

A dark path awaited them. Shrivelled mummies hung from the walls, keeping them company along the galleries. Vera pushed up her score as Clarissa and Lark fought against vermin, living mummies, mechanical artefacts, poisoned barbs and creatures of the night. What they did not expect was to encounter the invisible, that which eludes the senses. In itself indescribable, except for the brief awareness of its consequence.

The energy field which absorbed Lark was unforeseeable. Vera felt the discharge in her left-hand glove. To protect him she activated the last smart device Lark had left. Felix heard Vera's sharp cry when she saw Lark disintegrate inside the energy force he had just broken through. The blue light turned an incandescent orange on touching Lark's winged body. He had only just managed to turn and stretch his arm out to Clarissa, his hand outside the energy field. A few seconds before disintegrating as if he had never existed. Clarissa was surrounded by the same light. She closed her eyes awaiting the same fate. The shielding force field had been Lark's last act. Activated with the ring on his saving hand he enveloped Clarissa in a veil of protective light. Lark had saved her.

'Vera, are you all right?' Felix could hardly remain detached. The retinal projection only allowed him to see the changing images of the surroundings. Landscapes and settings advanced at the speed of Lark's and Clarissa's movement. Default beings and characters, figures which appeared and disappeared according to the need to destroy them in order to proceed. Felix was only able to imagine the avatars' actions, invisible to him. Clarissa and Lark moved as a projection on Vera's retina. When he saw her take off the glove, Felix knew that Vera had lost Galo's Lark.

Shrouded by the protective light, Clarissa crossed the energy field. She had completed the last of the challenges in the catacombs. The 'surprise option' had earned her hundreds of points, allowing her to advance.

She fell curled up at the foot of the wall of St Peter's Basilica. To gain access through the wall would allow her entry into the secret room. If Vera recovered from the loss of Galo, Clarissa would manage to pull herself together and act fast. She knew her emotions had been a hindrance when the time came to save Lark. The fire which had burnt his wings had been fed by her distress at the prospect of losing him. Once more she had to put her emotions on hold. Against Vera's will, Clarissa's body seemed to retain the impressions of the previous moment. Forging ahead was not what she wanted to do. The lack of meaning was making itself felt in her flesh. She was paralysed by the thought that the virtual loss was as real as what she had lived through. She had no time to waste, not even seconds. Vera gave out a yell full of urgency to dispel her immobility. This time it sounded to Felix like a combative shout rather than a shout of despair. Clarissa uncurled in a single movement which set her on her feet. She felt the wall to find the access mechanism. The Swiss Guard's footsteps could be heard ever more clearly.

Felix gathered that this was the final stage. They did not have much time. The alarm to vacate the building had been set off. The vocal warning was repeated every twenty seconds. Instructions by the female voice sounded soothing in the recorded message of controlled alert. Through the window Felix could hear the voices of security staff and police from the lower courtyard. He looked out of the window. They were scanning the staff's PECs two by two and he imagined the evacuation of the building would take time. A few minutes? He heard doors opening on the lower floors. They had presumably sent guards to check each office.

The secret entrance opened onto the inner corridor. The Swiss Guard was turning the corner with the weight of the wall closing in on his footsteps. Clarissa slid her body around it to enter the corridor without being seen. She waited with her ear to the wall until the sound on the other side had disappeared. She took one of the torches from the inner wall. She had advanced only a few steps when she stopped short. She was at the door to the Basilica's secret room. At last she would be able to access the Holy Book.

Why had she stopped? She should enter right away. Two guards patrolled the circular corridor in opposite directions eventually to meet in front of that very entrance. Clarissa's eyes pierced her retina. What else could Vera do, if not lead her towards the final moment? Clarissa remained immobile as if it were not Vera controlling her movements. Was it possible for an avatar to resist acting out their role? She knew very well Clarissa was not an independent being, but she was not sure whether it was she herself who had frozen. Clarissa stared at her blankly. Her eyes met Vera's as if to say to her: what now? She was at the door which would finally enable her to reach catharsis. She had arrived at the place where she would confirm the truth. It was not enough. Vera felt a stab. As if a fine needle of light cut through their mutual gaze, reflected in a perfect circle on her own retina. What now? She closed her eyes when she felt the stab. When she opened them again, Clarissa was already on the other side of the door. The guards had just positioned themselves in front of the entrance which Clarissa had crossed thanks to the master key in her boot. From the high gallery surrounding the enclosure she leant out to look at the room. It was not luxurious or even big but basic and functional. An iron staircase descended to the centre where the chest was resting on a pedestal. She started climbing down the stairs oblivious to the two pairs of fiery eyes that followed her movements from the darkness behind the railings facing the chest. Vera got a bigger fright than Clarissa when the double growling coming from the dribbling jaws broke into the silence. The two heads of the mastiff went through the bars so close to

Clarissa that Vera could smell their reeking breath. For now that was just a warning. They went back to the darkness and Vera to the task in hand.

Clarissa no longer looked her in the eye. Her gaze circled the room following the walls covered in hieroglyphs. Once again Clarissa stopped. Her perception was Vera's perception. More than ever they had to be one to succeed. This time Vera understood what it meant. Clarissa had managed to catch her attention. Now she must do what she knew best. It was the right place and time to act.

'New code. In there. That's it,' the words only audible to herself. 'Felix!'

'Tell me. I'm right here next to you.'

'I'm going to write new code. When I tell you, you must substitute it. You must be ready to do so at exactly the right time.' Vera knew that Clarissa would only get one chance. On entering the secret enclosure the chest with the Holy Book would open only once. If she managed to open it, she could see its contents. That would be the final epiphany to reach catharsis. Vera used the last control device left to her. She pressed standby. She had five minutes to write the substitute code. There was no need to remove the mind-corrupting code. All she had to do was write its replacement.

'I'm coming out.'

'Vera, there's no time.'

'I know I'll soon see what's embedded in *Cf*. Once I've written the code you must substitute it when I tell you to,' Vera repeated the instructions.

This time Felix understood he had to let her act. From the back of the room he saw the 3D images of the secret enclosure freeze. Without removing the glove, Vera opened a small window on the screen. She began to write.

Before leaving the enclosure, Clarissa would have to put back the book and seal the chest. Otherwise the two-headed mastiff would burst through the railings. It guarded the knowledge in the Holy Book, which had to remain in the enclosure. Clarissa would be granted just one opportunity to absorb that knowledge. At the end of the road she had no further ally or weapon options left. She would not be able to save herself from its jaws. Either of them would rip her head off in a single bite. If Clarissa did not reach the end, Vera would have no hope of replacing the code. With the security guards nearby, the moment for enacting her plan would have passed.

Once again Vera picked up pace, running her fingers over the screen, more confident than ever with the certainty that Clarissa had helped her reach, or she Clarissa. The silence was intense. The depth of the moment in all its enormity. Clarissa descended the stairs expecting a trap, sensing a raid. When she stepped off the last step and had both feet on the black marble floor of the enclosure, it seemed as if the walls were caving in on her. She evaded the pieces of hieroglyph which were flying around haphazardly until she realised that they were not lumps of brick or stone falling off the walls, but pieces of paper. They fell on the floor like rain, peeling off in thousands of fragments. The clarity of the stripped walls revealed the next task. The chest would only open once Clarissa had put the hieroglyphs together again. Like a jigsaw on the walls.

On its own, the concentration required to complete this task would be enough to put anyone into a trance. Vera had the speed of a coding expert. When she resumed the game, the window no longer framed the exterior darkness. The timid reflection of the moon was creeping in to reveal the shiny perspiration on her face. Felix was beset by a growing sense of powerlessness. Perhaps he should abort the game. Although Vera no longer communicated with him, he imagined she was in difficulty. If he disconnected her he might cause her greater harm.

'Vera, at least give me a sign that you're all right.' Felix waited what seemed like an eternity, although it was no more than a few minutes. Vera did not relieve his anxiety. She had no way of responding. What Felix and Vera had speculated upon was now materialising in the flesh. Vera had fallen into a trance.

Clarissa lifted the heavy book in both hands. The emanation escaping the chest did not seem to affect her. It was Vera who felt the drowsiness in her face, preventing her from operating the controls or changing direction. If she wanted to get as far as Galo had managed to, she should not resist. She was at the mercy of the game. She let herself be led by her stupor. Vera could not even recognise where she was. She was now in a hypnotic state. What followed was the only thing that became as crystalline as it was unalterable.

Out of the darkness of the chest the silver embossed letters on the cover clearly stood out. *The Bible*. When Clarissa began flicking through the scriptures, everything stopped. The two-headed mastiff stood as if turned to stone. Clarissa began to read. '*...Let us make man in our image, in our likeness, so that they may rule over the fish of the sea and the birds of the air, over the livestock, over all the earth...*' The pages followed on one from the other and none could be skipped. '*...Cursed is the ground for your sake; in toil you shall eat of it all the days of your life... In the sweat of your face you shall eat bread until you return to the ground... For dust you are, and to dust you shall return... Jehovah saw that the evilness of man was rife in the world... he regretted making man... the children of Israel were fruitful, and increased abundantly, and multiplied, and the land was filled with them... midwives feared God... Every son that is born you will cast into the river... Jehovah hardened his heart... a plague... every firstborn shall die... laws... atonement of guilt... offerings... sacrifice...*' Clarissa absorbed human history thus revealed in hundreds of pages of the Holy Book. '*...every bed on which he sleeps shall be unclean...*

impurity... shall slit its throat... scatter its blood... keep my statutes... condemned... torn by beast... defiled... let none deceive his brother... walled city... they are my serfs... I will appoint over you terror... I will cut down your images... armies...' The harsh words continued to pile up, unyielding. Their narration foretelling disaster. *'...prophecies... the flame of the fire shall not be quenched, and all faces shall be burned therein... prediction... give the command.... scum... I shall gather you in my anger and in my fury...'* Just as suddenly as tender words appeared *'...we come to adore you... they rejoiced... came down like a dove...'*, damning words would re-emerge. *'...Repent... cut off your right hand... shall have no recompense... we threw out demons... because they were sinners... thrown to the fire... foolish man... ruin ...And they were judged each according to their works...'* In just a few minutes Clarissa reached the last page. Thus she read the scriptures to the end. *'Seal not the words of the prophecy in this book, for the time is nigh... If anyone adds to these things, God will add to him the plagues that are written in this book; and if anyone takes away from the words of the book of this prophecy, God shall take away his part from the Book of Life, from the holy city, and from the things which are written in this book.'*

The last sentence wrenched Vera from her stupor with the clarity of the precise moment for what she had to do. Felix was beside her, waiting. Vera again took control of the game.

When Clarissa lifted the book by its golden covers, the pages hung like the thousands of people condemned in its name. With a click Clarissa lit the flame. The dog barked furiously shaking its heads enraged by the fire burning over the chest, trying to find a way to get through the railings. The game would not release him while the book was still in the enclosure. The Holy Book was burning on top of the chest. The blackened covers were a crude representation of its already inexistent content. Before burning her fingers,

Clarissa dropped into the chest what remained of the charred volume, sealing its fate.

The book fell into the chest slowly as if gravity had vanished from the enclosure. Vera was approaching the end of the game.

'Felix! Now!'

Felix, holding the new code between his fingers ready to overwrite Daniel's code, dropped it almost simultaneously onto the screen. The code was replaced. He had no way of knowing what Vera and Clarissa could see before their eyes. For Felix the Bible remained intact in the chest. He could see it in the 3D images, which he followed engrossed in the darkness of the office. For Vera and Clarissa the lid of the chest was closing on the translucent wisp of smoke which emanated conclusively. The Holy Book's gold covers were buried in the chest. The Holy Book had been replaced. Clarissa had successfully completed level five. She had survived. Her cathartic process was just beginning.

When the chest closed, Felix knew Vera had completed the game. He no longer felt the same urgency while he checked the new code on the screen. Vera, on the other hand, felt as if she had been turned inside out like a glove.

What she experienced was neither of a brilliant white light, nor a whirl of cosmic flashes, nor an entry at the sound of speed. First it was only the weeping of consciousness. As though emerging from the maternal womb into the unknown universe that is the world. Just the emergence. With it, the pain of abandoning the protective, encapsulated world. Like a newborn baby girl Vera renewed her perception of the space around her. Seeing spaces in which she had never been before. Spaces so inexistent, they were real.

What Vera had been seeking had found her instead.

The dimension Vera entered had left behind the place where she had learnt to be. It could have been over months, or a mere second. In the infinity of cosmic expansion or the smallness of an atom. That place where her perception was, with neither time nor space. She perceived the mind in cells. She saw the atoms of her own body and viewed herself in space. She and space as one. With the beings she knew and those who were different but equally a part of her. She became aware of life in the common spirit. She saw life stretched out timelessly. Without opposites. Everything was the same and one. The invisible light had reached her as if nothing of herself existed. She found herself immobile in the universe, almost like the static lake where the only thing was to be. Where everything from the past and future was. There was Galo, in the living essence of the lake. Without seeing him, she felt his presence. Almost more real than if she were seeing him with her own eyes. Perhaps only a glimmer was all that was needed; so clear that there was no language that could express it. So strong and vast in its depth that it was not possible to know it in words. Mere seconds in Vera's life. An eternity in its true perception. Vera allowed herself to be known by an all-encompassing consciousness. It touched her to give her a hint of its light.

'Vera!' Felix managed to shout once, unable to prevent Vera from collapsing onto the frozen floor. When the guards entered using the master key, Felix was carrying Vera in his arms. He looked at them wordlessly and with the same concern they all stared at Vera's limp body. The lights switched on in the office dimmed the bright moonlight coming in through the window, a frame around the full moon.

When she opened her eyes, the light was too white and she had to squint to let them readjust. She managed to recognise her new friend's voice.

'Welcome back. How are you feeling?'
'I'm here.'

'I'm glad. You've been unconscious for hours.'

Little by little Felix's figure filled the white space of the hospital room. Appearing with greater clarity each time. Her eyes no longer stung. Felix drew the curtain half-closed.

EPILOGUE

The World Government had approved the investigation. For months it had discreetly been keeping a close eye on the global suicide rate. Once it hit fifty thousand, they had decided to designate a workgroup. Father Zillo's was among the main names of the investigating committee. The World Government's initial surprise on discovering that Zillo was also on the list of suicides was dispelled a few weeks later when recording his death as part of a triple crime of passion was the most convenient option. Just as the suicides had begun, they ceased overnight. The investigation was suspended until further notice. The draft observation and statistics document was archived internally. 'Detectable Dangers Affecting the Security for the Preservation of the Human Species.' Neither Carda nor Vera wanted to speculate whether the World Government had somehow been involved. The company was taken over by a new Director of Security. The alteration of the code from Vera's terminal was never mentioned. She was asked only to leave the company. In his statement to the police, Carda explained the outcome of the triangle between Zillo, Roch and Martino. Although Roch had filmed Zillo hundreds of times for the campaigns, Zillo personally controlled when and how his office was connected to the building's closed circuit. In spite of Zillo's instructions, no record was found of what had happened in his office. No one could picture the true events which had unfolded in that room on that night.

Felix took her by the arm as they walked along the beach.

'I knew it couldn't be a mistake. Firstly, the hypnotic element. As Daniel's document revealed. Then the message to program the right hemisphere. I had never imagined it would be the Bible.'

'Me neither.'

'I've never read it.'

'Me neither. Did you know what *Cf* stands for?' Vera had one more question for Felix.

'Zillo wanted something meaningful. *Corbona fidei*. I think it means in Latin something like 'treasure for the faith'.'

'It was in Daniel's code as the acronym for *chemin final*.

'Final path. This must have come from Zillo and his obsession with the French.

'Do you think it was deliberate? A mechanism to provoke suicide?'

'While you were unconscious I sat beside you flicking through the Bible. It's teeming with control patterns. From beginning to end it is governed by the fear of sin, punishment and the sentence in hell. I imagine the imposition of the Bible in the hypnotic state worked like a burden for users. The mechanism forced ideas from the brain's left hemisphere into the right.'

'That's clearly not where they should reside. I find it hard to believe that Zillo did not suspect there was a risk.'

'You're very understanding, bearing in mind that Galo was one of the victims.'

Felix knew when not to expect any reply.

'They found Daniel's body. Perhaps Zillo sensed the problem brewing and decided to get rid of him. I knew him rather too well, I'm afraid.'

'With Zillo's death there are many things which will never be clarified.'

Felix continued to marvel at Vera's capacity to always leave a door open. They walked in silence for several long

232

minutes. It was not an oppressive silence as in the past. The place had much more to say to them. They reached the far side of the cove. Vera stopped when she noticed the bell tower in the distance.

'Before entering *Cf* you were repeating "rewotym". Yesterday too, before you regained consciousness. It was Galo's password, wasn't it? Does it mean anything?'

'It's "my tower" backwards.' Vera let go of his arm. 'I must go.'

'See you on-screen?' Felix smiled.

'Maybe.'

What Vera had experienced was neither exceptional nor superhuman. It was as human as it was natural even though her memory of it could only interpret her epiphany in the same way dreams are deciphered. With the limited comprehension of consciousness. What she went through was not yet in line with what was known as part of the psyche. Now that her moment of epiphany had ended, the profound feeling of detachment that Vera felt was alleviated by the certainty that it had been true.

She had thought about the past. Like a solid mass it consisted of events she could not alter. Galo's death now took on a different dimension. It no longer disheartened her. The fragility of the minds Zillo had tried to control had transpired to have great strength. Although it was in the most tragic manner, those minds had refused to be controlled. By evading the programmed dependency they had pierced its truth. Along the way, they had come to know the angst of being which they had ignored.

Vera understood the profound meanings revealed to her. Almost linked to astral rhythms. To the internal beat of the Earth. Vera learnt one thing above all else. Nothing had happened by chance. Coincidences were hugely significant negligible synchronicities. Everything linked almost inexplicably, but real. With eyes veiled over, centuries of synchronicities could pass without being seen. It was they that ordered chaos, showed the way, offered the choice. Even if unseen, nothing would stop anyway. Time would carry on regardless. The meaning of life would run free. Each time more so. Unaware that nobody could see it. Such as the apparently unconnected interstices of the universe.

While somewhere in the silence, life made infinitesimal links to signs, their purpose and their breath. Events breathing each other until they touched on being. Open, coordinating participation of its principles. Vera had reached the very limits of the possibility of being. She had stretched into the purpose of the natural cycle. She had touched possibility.

The world went on as it was. Where it was heading was predictable for a few. Where it might go continued to be a dark pit for most, like a secret nobody wants to know. What Vera had seen had changed her for ever. Her path, although solitary, showed her what was possible. Now she only needed to find out how.

She was glad the landscape she remembered had not changed. She was glad that on that side of the world the same tranquillity seemed to reign over everything. From the bell tower, Vera once again viewed the same horizon that had offered her meaning. There she sat until the moon appeared. It was bright like no other, closer than ever. From the starry sky the moon followed her slow steps, as it watched Vera walk across the vegetable garden and disappear into the convent building.

GLOSSARY

PEC   Personal Electronic Card
SRD   Sensitive Response Device
HUD   Heads Up Display
SON   Self-Organizing Network
ABD   Anomalous Behaviour Detection
IPS   Intrusion Prevention System
PEF   Personal Electronic File